Lady Wallac, Elise Polko

Reminiscences of Felix Mendelssohn-Bartholdy

A Social and Artistic Biography by Elise Polko

Lady Wallac, Elise Polko

Reminiscences of Felix Mendelssohn-Bartholdy
A Social and Artistic Biography by Elise Polko

ISBN/EAN: 9783337014377

Printed in Europe, USA, Canada, Australia, Japan

Cover: Foto ©Raphael Reischuk / pixelio.de

More available books at **www.hansebooks.com**

REMINISCENCES

OF

FELIX MENDELSSOHN-BARTHOLDY

A

SOCIAL AND ARTISTIC BIOGRAPHY

BY

ELISE POLKO

TRANSLATED FROM THE GERMAN

BY

LADY WALLACE

WITH

ADDITIONAL LETTERS ADDRESSED TO
ENGLISH CORRESPONDENTS

NEW YORK
LEYPOLDT & HOLT
1869

MUSICAL LITERATURE.

—

BEETHOVEN'S LETTERS.   1 vol., 16mo...................$2 00
MOZART'S LETTERS.   2 vols., 16mo...................... 3 00
MENDELSSOHN'S LETTERS.   2 vols., 16mo.............. 3 50
LIFE OF MENDELSSOHN,   1 vol., 16mo................. 1 75
LISZT'S LIFE OF CHOPIN.   1 vol., 16mo................ 1 50
POLKO'S MUSICAL SKETCHES.   1 vol., 16mo........... 1 75
POLKO'S REMINISCENCES OF MENDELSSOHN.   1 vol...... 1 75
MOZART: A BIOGRAPHICAL ROMANCE.   1 vol., 12mo.... 1 50
THE MUSICAL ART PRINCIPLE.   1 vol., 16mo.........   40

The above (with the exception of the last two) are all beautifully bound in uniform style, with gilt top and side-stamp, and form together a handsome little *Musical Library*.   They will be sent by mail, post paid, on receipt of the advertised price.

—

IN PREPARATION.

EHLERT'S LETTERS ON MUSIC.

ROBERT SCHUMANN'S WRITINGS ON MUSICAL LITERATURE.

LA MARA'S ESSAYS IN MUSICAL BIOGRAPHY AND CRITICISM.

—

LEYPOLDT & HOLT, *Publishers,*

451 BROOME ST., NEW YORK.

—

Additions of the best Musical Literature will be made from time to time, uniform in style with the letters of Mendelssohn, etc.

PREFACE

BY THE TRANSLATOR.

In presenting to the public an English version of Madame Polko's "Reminiscences of Mendelssohn," the Translator feels assured that it will be gladly welcomed, from the sympathy felt in every detail connected with that illustrious Master. Some valuable letters hitherto unpublished, and written in English, are added to those collected by Madame Polko, contributed by the kindness of Mrs. Mounsey Bartholomew, the widow of Mr. Bartholomew, who wrote the English *libretti* of the "Elijah," "Athalie," "Antigone," "Œdipus," and many other works of Mendelssohn.

The Secretary to the "Harmonic Society," Mr. Brewer, has been so good as to contribute three letters on the subject of the first performance of the "Elijah," by that Society; and to the family of the late Mr. Joseph Moore, the public are indebted for a correspondence on the subject of the Birmingham Festivals of 1840 and 1846.

Dr. Sterndale Bennett has authorized the publication of a letter from M. Ferdinand David, written at the time of the gifted Master's lamented death.

The letter to Mr. Novello was lithographed at the time, or private circulation, but, being comparatively little known, it is included in this collection. The one addressed to Madame Ertmann is extracted from " Die Ton-Halle," a musical paper, in which it recently appeared. It is the only one written in German.

The extracts from a correspondence with the late Mr. Coventry, on the subject of Sebastian Bach's Organ Sonatas, are of much interest.

PREFACE.

I HAVE attempted in this little work to furnish a kind of commentary on the precious legacy of Mendelssohn's Letters, and likewise a sketch of his biography, the full completion of which is, we are told, to be reserved for a later period. The materials consist of written and spoken details gathered from the dearest friends of the departed one, and also from the reminiscences of a girl, at that time very young, in whose life the appearance of the ever-memorable Mendelssohn formed a brilliant epoch. Particular dates are taken from the sketches by Wilhelm Lampadius, which appeared immediately after the death of Mendelssohn.

However kindly my applications for information were received wherever I sought it, and however great the readiness and amiability that supplied me with the hitherto unpublished letters of Mendelssohn in the Appendix, still I soon saw, with all my devotion to the work I had undertaken, the inexpressible difficulty of collecting correct and minute details on the subject of one so recently vanished from our sight, and of verifying such communications. By how many kindly scruples are survivors actuated!—how timidly are questions with regard to the deceased both asked and answered! and, consequently, how restricted must that hand be, which would so gladly depict the exact resemblance of so noble and lovable a form, worthy to become the property of the world at large! This same reverent reserve that shrinks from lifting the folds of that mysterious veil which the hand of the Angel of Death casts here below over departed humanity, has caused many a delicate trait that I would fain have preserved, to be effaced in this portrait.

Although the eyes of those who had the happiness of standing in nearer relationship with the departed one may discover shortcomings and deficiencies in this picture, and some-

times miss a certain blending of color, *one*
thing at least *all* must and will acknowledge—
that it is painted *con amore* in the fullest sense
of the phrase.

ELISE POLKO.

MINDEN, February, 1868.

CONTENTS.

REMINISCENCES OF MENDELSSOHN

CHAPTER I.

INTRODUCTION—YOUTH.

Methinks my listening spirit hears
Sweet melody of chiming bells!

THE chimes of remembrance are this day
ringing in my heart, and it is amidst their
sounding and ringing that I take up my pen
to write this little book. It is a woman who
here speaks of a great departed one, and whose
head and hand attempt for the first time to
delineate him. Not that we either are, or aspire to be, historical painters. We are minia-
ture painters, and do not pretend to execute
frescoes in a grand style; most frequently, we
either sketch in crayons, or paint on ivory, and
yet the world is compelled to admit, in our
praise, that we succeed in seizing the most
delicate contours of a head, and in reproduc-

ing its softest tints and most tender lines. Many rooms have not space enough for a life-sized portrait; while a little sketch, or a medallion, everywhere finds a niche, like a flower placed within the leaves of a song or prayer-book, in memory of the bright summer-time, when it first bloomed.

FELIX MENDELSSOHN-BARTHOLDY.

On the 8th of February, 1824, old Zelter, in Berlin, wrote to Göthe :—" Yesterday, Felix's fourth Opera, with dialogue all complete, was performed by us.   There are three acts, which, including two ballets, occupy about two hours and a half.   The work was very well received. In my poor judgment, I cannot master my astonishment that a boy, only just fifteen, should advance with such rapid strides.   Everywhere we find novelty, beauty, originality—thorough originality—intellect, facility, repose, euphony, completeness, dramatic power, and the solidity besides of an experienced hand. The orchestra interesting, neither oppressive nor wearisome, but merely forming an accompaniment. The musicians play it with good-will, and yet it is by no means easy. What seems familiar to our ear comes and passes away, not as a plagiarism, but as welcome and appropriate in its place—sprightliness, vivacity without haste, tenderness, refinement, love, passion, simplicity. The overture is a singu lar composition, reminding one of a painter who dashes colors on his canvas, and then works away at the mass, with his brush and his fingers, till at length a group comes to light, so full of truth, that in surprise you strive to discover what incident had occurred to produce it. I speak, indeed, like a grandfather who spoils his grandchild ; but I well know what I am saying, nor have I said anything that I cannot prove. First of all, by the ample praise bestowed on it, best tested by its reception from the members of the orchestra and the singers, in whom we can quickly discern whether coldness and repugnance, or love and good-will, inspire their fingers and their throats. You must know what I mean. As words of sympathy please him to whom they are addressed, so is it with the composer who places before the performer what he can succeed in, and who with equal enjoyment imparts it to others. I think this thoroughly explains it all."

In the autumn of this same year, Ignaz Moscheles gave his first concert in Berlin. He came from London, where he was highly esteemed, and had been induced to take up his abode. A vast reputation preceded this virtuoso and composer, scarcely yet thirty years of age; the excitement to hear him was very great, and the *élite* of an elegant and musical society filled the hall. Moscheles played Bach, Beethoven, Mozart, and lastly, a pianoforte Concerto in E-flat major, of his own composition. This celebrated artist caused an extraordinary sensation by his finished execution and admirable rendering. Among his hearers was a boy of fifteen, who, in breathless excitement, followed every passage and every note. His handsome face was flushed, his dark eyes sparkled with enthusiasm. It was Felix Mendelssohn-Bartholdy.

In spite of all his watchfulness, he occasionally cast a bright glance at a tall man with a genuinely musical forehead, who never failed to respond to his eager look by a smile and nod of sympathy. Though evidently a stranger, this personage appeared to be the object of much observation. Indeed, when Moscheles had finished playing, he at once went up to him, and, holding out his hand, asked him in a cordial tone, "Are you satisfied, Herr Kapellmeister?" "Satisfied! my dear friend, allow me to embrace you. You played gloriously!" It was the far-famed Hummel, from Petersburg, on his way to Paris, who said these words, and thus heartily admired his young colleague. After the concert, a select circle of congenial souls assembled at the Mendelssohns' house, where there was a gay supper given in honor of Hummel and Moscheles; and surely the round table, where those guests now banqueted, was not a less illustrious one than that of King Arthur of old. The two principal guests sat beside the respected host and the intellectual hostess. The other celebrities were

Zelter, Berger, Bernhard Klein, Robert (the two last accompanied by their young and handsome wives), and likewise the four blooming children of the family—Fanny, Felix, Rebecca, and Paul. All were so gay and animated during supper, that even the delicate pensive face of Ludwig Berger brightened. Hummel, who, when with those sympathetic to his nature, was the most cheerful and witty of men, could not fail to feel thoroughly at home here, where dazzling flashes of wit played around the golden wine. Amusing adventures of artists and incidents of travel were related, and hearty laughter resounded, while they chatted on, devoid of all restraint. Suddenly Felix rose, and gliding round the table to his father, whispered a few words in his ear; he nodded kindly in assent; and when the boy returned to his place, in the midst of the universal gayety, he raised his glass, exclaiming in an excited voice, "To the health of the composer of the E-flat major Concerto!"

At a late, very late hour, they all repaired to the music-room. Who could have felt weary in such society! The presence of the one stimulated the other. At the sight of the pianoforte and music-desks, the conversation took a higher flight. The most important subjects connected with art, and their beloved music, formed the sole topic from that moment. Bernhard Klein, just returned from 'a journey to Italy, spoke with enthusiasm of the land of song, and of the musical treasures in the archives shown to him by the Papal Kapellmeister Baini. Meanwhile Zelter, with his rough bass voice, sang, to the universal delight of all present, "Sanct Paulus war ein Medicus;" Ludwig Berger, a player full of soul, attempted, in spite of his crippled arm, a movement from his new F major Sonata; Moscheles played an astonishing Bravura; and lastly, Hummel extemporized on a theme of Mozart's. Ludwig Tieck says, "Evening softens and melts the feelings, awaking presentiments and mysterious sensations in the artist, who then more forcibly feels that beyond this life there exists within him another, more fruitful in art; and his inner genius often spreads its wings, from the longing to attain freedom, and to take flight into the land that lies behind the golden clouds of evening."

It was emotions such as these that vibrated in the playing of Hummel's lofty yearning spirit on that evening. During all this wondrous variety of performances, the handsome boy, in a jacket, stood modest and motionless beside the piano, a worthy study for a painter. His delicate features lit up with inspiration, he listened with burning cheeks, while his eyes never quitted the hands of the players.

At the close of Hummel's enchanting Fantasia, old Zelter, suddenly breaking in on the tender mood that had taken possession of the company, placed his hand on the shoulder of his young pupil, saying playfully, "Come, Felix, show now what you have learned, and do some credit to us, your teachers. Sit down and play whatever comes into your head."

The stranger guests eagerly urged compliance with this proposal, and the boy was assailed on every side; but he became paler and paler; and at last, with imploring looks, declared most positively that he would not play. A refusal of this kind was unprecedented, and excited great surprise. "What on earth is the matter with you, boy?" exclaimed Zelter, in his uncouth fashion; "are you going to show the white feather, after playing fearlessly in grand concerts, and before our Göthe in Weimar? What must I write to him about you?—that you have become a poltroon?" "Oh! at that time I did not rightly know what I was doing," answered Felix, in a faltering voice; "but now I can only say that, after those two there," glancing with swimming eyes at Hummel and Moscheles, "I neither can, nor ought to play," and, bursting into a flood of tears, he rushed out of the room.

Next morning, Moscheles received a charming note from Frau Mendelssohn, in which she earnestly entreated him to give instructions on the piano, during his stay in Berlin, to her two eldest children, Fanny and Felix, and thus to fulfill the eager longing of the boy, who, since the previous evening, had perpetually dreamt of the E-flat major Concerto; and she added: "Felix begs me urgently to ask you to allow him to see that composition, as he is so anxious to ascertain how those difficulties that so greatly excite his surprise can be executed."

Moscheles, forthwith, sent the MS. to his youthful admirer, with a few kind words, and the assurance that it would give him peculiar pleasure to superintend the musical studies of himself and his sister. He at the same time appointed an hour on the following day when they might examine together the E-flat major Concerto.

That hour arrived, and Felix received his new teacher with a face beaming with delight; and, seating himself at the piano, he played the Concerto, to the astonishment of the listener, in such a fiery and spirited manner that it brought tears into the eyes of the composer. The boy occasionally interrupted his playing, to repeat first one passage and then another of particular difficulty, asking Moscheles, with modest anxiety, whether he was satisfied with his mode of executing it. The latter, however, could only embrace the player in cordial delight.

The alliance now concluded between these two artistic natures was destined to last for life. Moscheles was strongly attracted by the boy, and the instruction he gave him and his clever sister Fanny interested him so much, that, instead of weeks, he remained months in Berlin, a daily guest of the Mendelssohn family—and what a family it was! Göthe, says, "That man is the most fortunate who, whether a king or of more humble origin, finds happiness provided for him at home;" and if ever a "fortunate man" reaped such happiness in its fullest measure, it was Felix Mendelssohn-Bartholdy. His home was pervaded by an atmosphere of love and peace, as well as by the highest intellectual culture, in which the pinions of a youthful soul must wax strong, and every talent be developed in untarnished brightness.

"In his gay early youth, Mendelssohn wrote a vast deal; though his labors were not toilsome, but rather like the unintermitting yet natural growth of buds and blossoms, while the sun that matured this growth and increase was—*his parental home.* Ever blessed be such a home! No better talisman can be found against the perils of the journey of life, for man or woman, than the memories of a *loving home* —of the sweet and incomparable happiness once our portion there. Such remembrances are stronger than the golden links of the chain on the falcon's foot, that hold him fast when he would fain take flight—they gently, but surely, draw us back from far distant lands into our parents' house. Such memories inspire us with strength and courage; such a home is our earthly paradise—the only one here below from which we cannot be driven out. May a blessing, then, rest on those beloved ones who prepared for us, once on a time, that happiness which no other human beings, however loving or gentle, can ever again bestow on us—our father and mother! . . . Even at that time an infinitely rich spiritual and musical life ex-isted in the house of the Mendelssohn family, where the *élite* both of artists and lovers of art met ; the most brilliant names in science, art, and literature were represented there. How often the two Humboldts came, Varnhagen, Heine, and those young violin virtuosos, Rietz and David !—and, in addition, an ever-blooming *Flora* of the most attractive and fascinating fair forms, and among these the still wondrously beautiful Henriette Herz. The works of Felix were all here first carefully performed ; it was esteemed an honor and a privilege to be permitted to take a part in any musical performance at these celebrated Sunday *matinées ;* choruses and quartetts were sung ; quintetts and trios executed in rare perfection ; and it was on one of these Sunday forenoons that Moscheles played for the first time, with the most rapturous applause, his "Hommage à Händel." The young teacher and his talented scholar, moreover, played together daily for hours, discussing their mutual works, vying with each other in composing, arranging domestic concerts, and taking long walks. Felix showed the most grateful devotion and the most lively admiration of Moscheles, without, however, in the slightest degree neglecting, in favor of his new friend, those teachers who had hitherto instructed him. He possessed in a high degree the rare and pleasing virtue of *courtesy of heart*. His intercourse with Zelter and Berger was cordial and filial, submissive to their peculiarities, obedient to their will, and modestly subordinate to them in all things; tearing up at once, without a sigh, those compositions pronounced by Zelter or Klein to be insignificant, thus no doubt depriving us for ever of many a charming piece of music. Those, too, who saw him, with the most cheerful air in the world, devoting himself for hours to the invalid Berger, and, in spite of his own sparkling vivacity, reading to him, playing and copying music for him, must have more than *admired*, they must have *loved* him.

The year 1824 closes for Felix his home life, so pleasant and devoid of cares. The first great and eventful interruption was a journey to Paris with his father, to see Cherubini, whose counsel was to be sought with regard to the future cultivation of the boy, and from whose own lips they wished to hear whether Felix had really a decided vocation for music. Felix Mendelssohn's finely-chiseled face, always the faithful mirror of his excitable soul, might well turn pale when he stood in the presence of the composer of the "Wasserträger," in order to play before him, with the celebrated Baillot, his G minor Quartette. Cherubini's kindly smile and warm praise were a reward that made the young virtuoso happy beyond measure, and decided his future profession in the eyes of his father. It was the same quartette which he played on his way from Paris, at Göthe's house in Weimar, and with regard to which the Poet-Prince informed Zelter that "Felix produced his last quartette, to the astonishment of every one. This audible and intelligible dedication pleased me much." A "Liebesschreiben" was enclosed in this letter for his friend's youthful scholar, in return for which Felix later sent him a masterly translation of the "Andrea" of Terence.

During the two following years he worked

much and hard. Etudes were written, a Symphony-Overture, and a Capriccio that his sisters and his brother playfully christened "Absurdité;" the most brilliant fruit of this period being the Overture to the "Midsummer Night's Dream."

The young artist now entered the University, where he studied indefatigably, attended Hegel's lectures, practised all chivalrous exercises, and continued, as ever, by his bright cheerfulness and amiability, the sun of the house and the idol of his family. The gay student was daily to be seen with a portfolio under his arm, a student's cap on his dark curly hair; and yet, in spite of all his earnest efforts, he had still sufficient time and humor to mimic inimitably, for the amusement of his brother and sisters, many a professor with "pendent queue," and others besides. In spite of all this, books of songs were written, as well as quartettes and sonatas, and the "Wedding of Camacho" was performed in the family circle. Meanwhile, an expedition to Stettin took place, where they were desirous to have Mendelssohn's newest orchestral works. Repeated performances were also given of Bach's "Passionsmusik," in the Berlin "Akademie," where, amazed at the steady security of the young conductor, scarcely twenty years of age, they sang and played even better than under the iron hand of Zelter himself. During this productive winter, the apparition of Paganini was first seen in Berlin; and that most marvelous of all artistic phenomena could not fail to make the most powerful impression on Mendelssohn, who poured out all his enthusiasm, astonishment, and enchantment in an excited letter to Moscheles.

At the close of his University studies, Felix set out on the journey that had so long occupied his thoughts—an artistic visit to Moscheles in London. A few days before the separation from his family, and for the consolation of his beloved and anxious mother, he composed his fascinating Overture, "Meeresstille und glückliche Fahrt."

A pleasing group no doubt assembled round the piano when Felix (who invariably submitted all his creations first to the criticisms of his family) played "Meeresstille." Who can tell whether that charming painter, Hensel, Fanny's betrothed, may not have sketched the scene ?—the brilliant eyes of his sisters over-looking the player, Fanny's delicate hand turn-ing the pages, Paul standing beside his mother near the instrument, and the father reclining with a glad face in his arm-chair. Even the most solicitous mother's heart might calmly intrust her beloved son to *that* glassy sea, for

> Athwart the ocean wilderness,
> No token of a wave.

At length, with the anxious mariner, we seem to long for a breeze; and presently, how im-perceptibly it ripples the waters, how gently it swells the sails, how playfully it drives on the vessel over the blue expanse, more and more rapidly.

> Quick ! Quick !
> Already I see land.

Thus the chorus joyfully sings—the loved one has reached the haven — Felix rises — the mother smiles, but tears stand in her fine eyes.

Felix took with him to London a rich store for his revered friend and teacher, Moscheles—the MS. of a sacred Cantata on a chorale, a fifteen-part Hora, and his first stringed Quartette.

The youthful traveler was received with open arms in Moscheles' house. The young lovely wife of his friend, only sixteen, whose whole character and disposition bore the impress of the most noble feminine nature, greeted him on the threshold with sisterly cordiality; a circle of eminent men—Klingemann among others, that poet so full of soul—welcomed him rejoicingly.

Those were bright days and sunny weeks that he passed in "merry old England." Felix at that period made his first appearance before a London audience. At a concert crowded to the door, the Overture to the "Midsummer Night's Dream," was given. Henriette Sontag, that lovely grace, that fascinating *salon* nightingale, consented to let her sweet voice be heard, and Mendelssohn played his Concerto in E major for two pianos with Moscheles. Nowhere is it recorded which of these three chosen *German* spirits excited the loudest storm of applause; it was indeed a rare combination of the great and the beautiful.

Mendelssohn's manner and appearance won all hearts. He was then in all the "storm and stress" period of youthful freshness, so keenly susceptible to all impressions; he went about with open eyes and an open heart, and nothing appeared more attractive in him than that genuine and admirable artistic modesty, which, ever aspiring to the highest aims, can never satisfy itself. The most tender friendship was formed between him and Klingemann, with whom he had been previously acquainted in Berlin—a refined noble nature and a thoroughly kindred soul. In his letter he addresses him as "My *one* friend." It is a charming test of Mendelssohn's heart, that all the friendships he ever formed endured to the end of his life, and his interest in those whom he had ever loved was never affected by time or space, but continued in all its fullness and strength to the last. How many voices could confirm this!

From London, Mendelssohn took a journey with Klingemann to Scotland, the grand and noble scale of its scenery exciting his enthusiasm, and detaining him longer than was either expected or wished for in London and Berlin. Whether the lustrous eyes of the lovely Scottish Queen held him spell-bound in Holyrood, or the magic power of Fingal's Cave —*chi lo sa?* He returned intoxicated with delight, while melodies innumerable floated in his head and in his heart.

The letters he addressed to Moscheles after his return to Berlin, on the subject of this his first great artistic journey, and which are to this hour in the hands of the venerable Master, cherished by him as an unapproachable and sacred treasure, are so full of delight with all he saw and enjoyed, so charmingly thankful, so gay and attractive with their familiar "thou," that we would fain bestow them on the world at large, like the fragrance of roses, or the sight of a bed of flowers in the morning sun.

How much had Felix to say to his beloved

ones at home!—and it was thus that the romantic legend of Fingal's Cave was brought to life and assumed its present form.   One day, Rebecca said, " Describe the fairy to us ! " while Fanny playfully added, " But it must be a long detailed story, to make us comprehend how and when it all occurred ! " on which Felix answered, " The legend cannot be described by commonplace words, and you know that I am no poet ; so I will play it over to you, and then you can tell me afterwards whether you saw and understood it all thoroughly."   Fair hands opened the well-loved instrument, and Mendelssohn played that wondrous legend subsequently called the " Overture to the Hebrides."   For my part, I always seem, amid all its sportive strains, to see Mary Stuart's enticing, alluring eyes, as they looked forth in bygone days from the ivy-mantled windows of the Palace of Holyrood, when listening to the tones of her faithful minstrel Rizzio's lute.

The journey to Italy took place in 1830-32. Thanks to the kind benefactors who bestowed on us the letters of that date, we are made closely acquainted with those sunny days. He who could lay down Mendelssohn's " Letters from Italy and Switzerland " without *sincere and heartfelt gratification*, without a sense of, I may say, *grateful* admiration of this richly endowed artistic nature, this *loving human soul*, is indeed as much to be pitied as the blind, who can see no spring, or the deaf, who can hear no nightingale's note.

Otto Gumprecht, in his clever article on Mendelssohn in " Unsere Zeit," says, with much truth and beauty, " The value of Mendelssohn's 'Letters,' which have gained for themselves a prominent place among the memoirs of chosen spirits, is by no means based on the fact that they bring before us in the most vivid reality the composer, in connection with the musical life of his day, as well as the development of the history of Art; not also merely on account of their rich fullness of thought, nor the breadth and variety of ideas they present to us at every step; far higher than all these is that lofty morality to be prized which impresses its stamp on all his revelations.

The life and character here unfolded would demand from us our warmest sympathy, even if he of whom it treats were not the creator of the music of the 'Midsummer Night's Dream,' 'The First Walpurgis Night,' and the 'Elijah.' In the writer of these letters, one of those gifted natures is unveiled, in presence of which we experience that pure delight, that elevating impression of the entire harmony between our preconceived idea and his actual being, which in most cases is only called forth by the contemplation of a work of art. We are here under the magic spell of an individuality, equally attractive and solid, displaying every side of humanity in its richest development, most harmonious proportions, and vivid reciprocal relations."

While we read Mendelssohn's letters, a succession of brightly-tinted pictures pass before us with a musical accompaniment. First of all, the form of the Weimar *Jupiter tonans*—courteous, dignified, amiable, inaccessible; next we are in the Munich Theater, seeing Schechner in " Fidelio; " then comes the amusing "day of misfortunes in the Bavarian Mountains," commencing with drawings torn up, and ending with the first bars of the A minor Symphony; the splendid Coronation of the King of Hungary in Presburg; *Venezia la bella*, with the female forms created by Giorgione and Titian; presently, " ecco Firenze," and at length Rome, Naples, Milan, Isola Bella, Switzerland. Paris and London form the close.

The genuine golden ground of all these pictures is that of *the heart*. We next find Mendelssohn manifested in a variety of ways in his relations to father, mother, sisters, brother, and brother-in-law, to his friends, to nature, and to the beautiful world of God; we are apt to think first of the *artist*, much as we rejoice in the *man*, and yet the two are, and ought to be, inseparable. They blend in the most consummate manner in these letters, and no line is anywhere perceptible to show where *the man* modestly withdraws, and the artist formally appears on the scene. It may perhaps be possible to write more learnedly, more brilliantly, or with more research, about Italy, but never with greater charm or warmth of heart!

No painter, no biographer, could give us such a graphic portrait of Felix Mendelssohn, or *so* faithfully record his inmost self, as he has himself unconsciously done in these letters. His eyes, as they look forth thence, are those genuine childlike, yet artistic eyes, akin to those of Raphael and Mozart, so rare in this world, and which can never be forgotten by those who have once seen them.   And yet we hear from his accomplished friend and traveling companion, Theodor Hildebrandt, various details of that delightful spring excursion that we would fain insert in the letters, as a commentary or supplement, which would reflect even a brighter light on this dear and noble man and artist.

We feel a certain degree of emotion when we hear that the two friends in Amalfi and Sorrento—in the presence of that singular and intoxicating magic world—read with delight and enthusiasm Jean Paul's "Flegel-Jahre," and that Mendelssohn would gladly have waited on his "Hillebart," or "Höllenbart," as Walt did on Wult; and how they also tried to sip tea, only to look at each other and to say, laughing, "*Tea?*—we are not ill surely?"

And then the *Saltarello* by moonlight, opposite the inn at Santa Lucia in Amalfi, and how Felix and the jovial painters danced, while all around was a marvel of beauty and brightness: and yet these are called the hours of *night*—and it was night in Amalfi. In the midst of the dancing, Mendelssohn called out to his friend, "Oh! that melody! mark it well, you shall find it again, in some shape or other, in a work of mine; that I am resolved upon." And Hildebrandt did find it again in a movement of the Fourth Symphony. "Now listen! that is a fragment of Italy. Don't you see the moon shining and the pretty girls dancing?" said Mendelssohn, when subsequently playing portions of his great work to his former traveling companion.

A water-color sketch, painted by Felix, of the inn of Santa Lucia, adorns Hildebrandt's album. "It is executed as if by the hand of our best water-color artists," said this competent judge. We first learn from the report of his painter friend, how deep and glowing was Mendelssohn's interest in the art of painting, and how rich his endowments in this respect also. It was no trifling play, no filling up of idle hours, no mere attempts; in every pursuit he was thoroughly in earnest, and, as in music, he exhibited in painting that industry and fiery zeal, which old Zelter, once in conversation with Hildebrandt, declared to be what he prized most highly of all in his Felix. "It is not his genius which surprises me and compels my admiration—for that he has from God, and many others have the same"—(thus spoke his attached teacher): "no, it is his incessant toil, his bee-like industry, his stern conscientiousness, his inflexibility towards himself, and his actual adoration of Art. He will gain a name in everything he undertakes."

In Rome, the family he most familiarly frequented was that of the banker, Anton Bendemann. Professor Julius Hubner was intimate there, and also one of Mendelssohn's friends.

The party who went together on an expedition to Naples and the Borromean Isles were: Director Schadow, with his wife and children, Karl Sohn, Eduard Bendemann, Theodor Hildebrandt, and Felix Mendelssohn.

How charming it sounds to hear of Felix seated at the piano, extemporizing one day in his apartment at Rome, when suddenly a splendid contralto voice repeated a theme out of his Fantasia. His friends, too, listened. It was a voice that had often met their ear in all its melody; the young maid of the landlady was in the habit of singing popular Italian airs during her work. On that day, however, Mendelssohn started up in surprise. "She sang my theme quite correctly!" exclaimed he. They opened the window; she was seated on the stairs singing, while packing all sorts of fruit into a large basket.

"Oh! if I could only once hear her sing near."

"Call her in, then."

"The question is, will she come?"

The painters were bolder than the musician,

and, after a short and playful negotiation, they persuaded her to come into the room. She was neither handsome nor graceful, and rather shy, but said she was willing to sing her songs. They hurried her to the piano, while the joyous companions grouped themselves in a circle, and the rare contralto voice rose before them like a calm moon. Mendelssohn accompanied her extempore as she sang. It must have been a rich picture and a rich enjoyment.

From that moment, Mendelssohn provided for the musical education of this girl in the most self-sacrificing manner, and the simple maid of the Piazza d'Espagna became an excellent singer. How often must she have remembered with deep gratitude the youthful benefactor, whose hand had led her out of obscurity into the bright warm light!

The " jovial companion," too, was not wanting in this parti-colored group; the gallant old General Lepel (who in Rome thought nothing worthy of notice except the situation of the " old hole ") lived in the same house. Thus it came to pass one day that Mendelssohn was extemporizing, and went on and on playing, without hearing or seeing what was passing near him; meanwhile His Excellency had come into the room, attired in a most comfortable dressing-gown, and remained standing behind the piano, till the player took his hands off the keys.

"Ah! your Excellency!"

"Good day, Felix. You did not perceive me, I suppose?"

"No! your Excellency."

"Singular enough, too, for I have been listening to you for some time. Now, Felix, don't fancy that I have any wish to be able to play on the piano like you—that would be beneath the dignity of a General—but do you know what I really should like? While standing here, I thought that if I chanced to be assailed by bad feelings, I should be glad to breathe them all away—so! so!—just as you have done in your strains." How often was this greatest of all praise from the lips of the old General playfully quoted by the friends?

Judging by the amount of songs to which

this poetical pilgrimage gave rise, the number of attractive ladies to whom they were doubtless offered in homage, seems to have been rather considerable—not forgetting to include the pious singing nuns in Rome, who inspired him with such a beautiful chorus for female voices. The fascinating Delphine Schauroth, and the gentle spiritual Josephine Lang, alone emerge distinctly out of the lovely chaos veiled in mist. Not less great, doubtless, was the *razzia* of hearts he pursued!

He was peculiarly susceptible to intellect, charm, and grace, but the groundwork of his whole being was here again a *golden ground*—that of the most profound and strict morality.

At cheerful social meetings, after the burden and heat of the day, at gay *fêtes*, the so-called "place of honor" repelled him, being often between two pretentious and high-born dames—*d'un certain âge*—who condescended with great affability to address the young musician. How quickly was he seized with a sudden attack of deafness, owing to the keen current of air that blew on this favored spot, and how soon he contrived to transfer himself to a place quite at the other end of the brilliant table, among all the young married women and girls, who received him as their idol, with joyous smiles and beaming glances!

A veil of profound melancholy rests on Mendelssohn's last letters. The tidings of Göthe's death, of that of Zelter, and of the friend of his youth, Rietz, the violinist, deeply affected him. His answers are all in the minor key. As to the impression made on him by the demise of his attached and renowned teacher, he writes: "On the day that I received the news of Zelter's death, I thought that I should have had a serious illness, and indeed during the whole of the ensuing week I could not shake off this feeling."

The memorable season in London, when he and Paganini shone as the most brilliant stars, did not suffice to obliterate the shadows of sorrow, his strongest impulse being to return to the warm atmosphere of the best of all love—a father's home.

On his return to Berlin, when the first

ecstasy of seeing and hearing each other once
more had subsided, Mendelssohn wròte repeatedly to Moscheles to persuade him to pay them
another visit, urging him also strongly to bring
his most charming wife. When his friend at
last agreed to come, Mendelssohn's joyful letter in reply began with a neatly written-out
trumpet *Fanfare.* He also inquired about a
Septette and Trio that Moscheles had recently
played in London to their mutual friend
Klingemann, and which had so enchanted him
that he had sent Mendelssohn a passage out of
it of fourteen notes, that he had retained in his
memory. "I should like to hear more of it,"
wrote Mendelssohn, "for those few notes are
perpetually in my head ; I seem to carry them
with me wherever I go."

When Moscheles actually arrived, accompanied by his wife, there was rejoicing without
end ; and those attached friends enjoyed four
weeks of the most delightful intercourse. The
far-famed master was received with great jubilation ; but however welcome such public rec-
ognition must have been to the artist, his inti-

macy with the Mendelssohn family gratified him still more. Fanny's wondrous talent enchanted him; Paul and Rebecca vied with each other in playing the violoncello; every evening there was music, and executed thoroughly *con amore*. In the bright days of autumn they made all sorts of expeditions together; in the afternoons they sang quartettes, composed by Felix in the morning, under the old trees in the garden; arranged clever little *fêtes* with fairy dances, and enjoyed to the uttermost being together, and the brightness of the present. The longed-for Septette and Trio were also played at that time, and forthwith arranged by Mendelssohn as duetts; and on the evening before his friend Moscheles' departure, he found the manuscript on the desk of the piano, Fanny and Rebecca having placed a wreath of China asters, gathered in the garden, on the music.

But the inexorable hour of farewell arrived at last :—

From this land we must sever,

as it is said in the song of the " Schifflein."

The Moscheles returned to London, but the
words "to meet again" crossed the sea on both
sides. This glorious autumn was unfortunately
followed by mists, hoarfrosts, and snow-storms
—a period of uncertainty, doubt, restlessness,
and a certain degree of irritation. The death
of Bernhard Klein, too, had imposed a new
burden of grief on Mendelssohn's heart. The
situation of Zelter, Director of the Academy
of Singing, for which Felix, the favorite pupil
of the great deceased teacher, had applied, by
the desire of his parents, was finally, after many
long and secret discussions, bestowed in December on the clever composer of the " Mort
d'Abel," Music-Director Rungenhagen, born
in 1788. It is said that the ladies' voices
turned the scale in this affair. It would have
been diverting to be behind the scenes when
this election was in progress ; what twittering,
fluttering, croaking, chirping, and piping in
every key ! One thing was certain, that the
nightingales, larks, blackbirds, thrushes, tit-
mice, chaffinches, swallows, and all the sing-
ing-birds voted for a *young* king ; whereas the

crows, magpies, crossbills, and, above all, the sparrows, insisted on having a mature master as their ruler; and it is said that *Berlin* sparrows present themselves more boldly, and maintain their rights more noisily, than sparrows in other places! Certain ladies, no longer, alas! counting their years by springs, but by winters, could not endure having a director whom they had carried in their arms as a child, and who, moreover, had the credit of a disagreeably correct memory. These fogs, however, were quickly dispersed; a nature such as Mendelssohn's could not long remain depressed by the failure of a hope, and so one day he writes to Pastor Bauer:—" When you think of me, do so as of a joyous musician who is doing *many* things, who is *resolved* to do many more, and who would *fain* accomplish all that can be done." The sun burst forth, spring looked down from the mountains—

> Balmy breezes are awaking,
> Soft melodious murmurs making;
> Into life each bud is breaking—
> New sounds, fresh fragrance day by day!
> Throbbing heart! thy pulses stay;
> The old hath passed away.

And at Whitsuntide, in June, 1833, Felix Mendelssohn stood on the threshold of a new and independent life, and long wished-for active occupation—at the director's desk in the Concert-Hall of Düsseldorf.

CHAPTER II.

DÜSSELDORF.

HEINRICH HEINE, in his "Reisebilder," says of this his native city :—" Düsseldorf is a town on the Rhine, where 16,000 people live, and where many a hundred thousand are buried. It is very beautiful, and longing feelings come over us when we think of it in distant lands."

When Mendelssohn arrived there, more than 16,000 people were assembled, not only because the cherished Whitsuntide feast had arrived, for it displayed a very different physiognomy from that it bore when that reckless but irresistible favorite of the Graces and Muses, Heinrich Heine, was still a pupil in the Franciscan cloister, and bought hot apple-tarts at the corner of the theater in the vicinity of the huge statue of the Elector. Düsseldorf had taken a grand upward flight since Wilhelm von Schadow took up his abode there, with a brilliant retinue of younger painters — Lessing, Hildebrandt, Sohn, Mücke, Hübner, Schirmer, soon to be joined by Bendemann and Steinbrück. In the long deserted rooms of the ancient castle—where Heine maintained that a lady in black silk, headless, and with rustling garments, nightly flitted about—easels now stood, and that work which "aspires to the beautiful" was begun, while pictures in their pomp of color bore the fame of the Düsseldorf school over all the world. Lessing painted his "Royal Couple;" Hildebrandt, his "Judith," ("Edward's Children" were sketched previous to the journey to Italy); Bendemann, the mourners "who sat by the waters of Babylon and wept;" Sohn, his beautiful "Hylas;" and Schirmer his profoundly poetical landscapes.

Immermann, the gifted poet, and his circle, formed the second court. He was at that very time sending forth into the world his "Tulifäntchen" to flutter there, which Heine so charmingly designates as an "epic humming-bird." In this society the most bright and prominent forms were the refined Gräfin Ahlefeldt, with her aristocratic attractions; the intellectual Elisabeth Grube; the fascinating poets Von Uechtritz and Zedlitz; the subtle investigator of art, Schnaase; and the original Grabbe.

In a remote cell of the academy, the walls of which were covered with clever sketches, were read aloud Hamlet, Wallenstein, Egmont, Romeo, the Standhaften Prinzen, the Opfer des Schweigens, Puss in Boots, King Œdipus, and many others, and there were held those model performances which created such a sensation, and in which Seydelmann appeared as a star.

Immermann, in writing about these hours in this cell, says:—"Beneath the window rushed the Rhine, while the white walls were reddened by the sun of spring. Within sound of the waves, in rosy light, syllables were measured, accentuation determined, and variety of tone in declamation worked out."

Beside these two radiant groups of painters and poets, a third musical one now appeared, and its brilliant center was—Felix Mendelssohn.

2*

A Whitsuntide Musical Festival! The words sound as genial as an A major chord. We feel the sunshine, we breathe the balmy breezes " steeped in blue," and inhale the fragrance of blooming lilacs. The founders of this grand and noble musical gathering, that, since 1818, brings, as it were, summer into the Rhenish spring, cannot fail to excite the warmest gratitude in the hearts of all those who ever assisted in the celebration of such a festival. Long processions of people come streaming in on every side from far and near, musicians and lovers of music; and above the door of every Rhenish concert-hall, at Whitsuntide, might fitly and justly be inscribed these lines :—

> Who can the sea of heads compute,
> Or who the names tell o'er?
> The hall with teeming multitudes
> Is crammed from roof to floor.

Not omitting to make honorable mention also of all the living flowers—varieties of roses, lilies, tulips, violets, pansies, forget-me-nots, ranunculuses—as well as a sprinkling of culinary herbs! It was, and still is, a display of

the most attractive forms, faces, toilettes, and
—voices withal. People go by turns to Cologne, Aix-la-Chapelle, Düsseldorf, and Elber-
feld, on these Whitsuntide days, to see and
to be seen, to listen and to admire, to play and
to sing.

Thus it once was, and thus it is to this day.

The concert programme of the Düsseldorf
Musical Festival, that Felix Mendelssohn directed for the first time, consisted of the following pieces :—

> " Overture in C major," by Mendelssohn ;
> Händel's " Israel in Egypt ; "
> " The grand Leonora Overture in C ; "
> Beethoven's " Pastoral Symphony ; "
> " Easter Cantata," by Wolf ;
> " Die Macht der Töne," by Winter ;

and, in addition, Mendelssohn played a Concerto of Weber's.   The soprano solos were sung
by the favorite of Berlin, the admired Pauline
von Schätzel-Decker, a friend of the Mendelssohn family.   Her sweet voice and her rendering, so full of soul, had the most enchanting
effect.

At the rehearsals, Mendelssohn's presence
had already excited the most lively interest.

How eagerly were all eyes, whether fine or the reverse, directed toward that slight form of middle height, his dark curling hair, his intellectual forehead, and well-chiseled mouth. And had this slender hand, almost feminine in its delicacy, with the conductor's *báton* in its grasp, power to control such masses of sounds and human beings? The result was awaited with excitement. But at the very first calm, modest words, with which he introduced himself, the mode of his address to the singers, in all its charming gayety of heart, produced the most pleasing impression in favor of the " Berliner."

When an hour had elapsed, the orchestra were playing with a fire and impetus such as they had never yet done, while the old musicians stole furtive glances of delight at the youthful director, muttering to each other, " He knows what he is about." The singers found that they might trust to him ; and as for the ladies ! *tace.*

The performance itself was a memorable one. The warm-hearted, excitable Rhinelanders seemed quite transported—applause, hurrahs, flowers, laurel-wreaths, sparkling eyes, flushed cheeks. They were determined to secure, at any cost, that masterly hand; so Mendelssohn was unanimously selected as City Music-Director, an appointment first created on his behalf, and, to the delight of all, he accepted this position for some years.

It was quite a matter of course that Mendelssohn should quickly feel himself at home in the Düsseldorf circles of that day. Notwithstanding all his devotion to his beloved art, no one came forward less as a one-sided musician than he. His brilliant and elastic spirit extended feelers on every side. All that was beautiful, great, and noble, in whatsoever form, attracted him, and engaged his eager attention. He had, indeed, in his parental home, been trained, not only to *hear*, but also to *see:* and eyes such as his had a quick perception of the beautiful. From his earliest youth, Lessing, Göthe, Schiller, Shakspeare, had been his friends, and everywhere he found ample time, from his ardent zeal, to exercise his remarkable talent for drawing, and to cultivate himself in every different branch. Gumprecht says, " An almost feminine tenderness of feeling, and a versatile imagination, fiery and impetuous in receiving impressions, are prominent peculiarities in Mendelssohn's individuality. But to these equivocal gifts of the gods was added an incorruptible understanding, purifying and strengthening him, and, most important of all, a determined and self-reliant character."

Innumerable passages in his letters prove how subtle was his sense of art, while every bar of his writings shows how full of poetry was his soul. The painters received him at that time as if one of their fraternity, and the somewhat exclusive circle of poets also gladly admitted him to share their privileges. He once more began to sketch and to paint with fresh zeal, and many captivating album pages, arabesques, and sketches, still extant in the hands of his various friends, testify how great was his talent, how correct his eye, how rich his fancy, and how graceful his hand. A most charming little pen-and-ink composition, in a letter to Moscheles, is of this date. Moscheles had written from London to Felix at Düsseldorf, to beg his young friend to stand godfather to his newly-born son. The whole orchestra, in a grand flourish of trumpets, rejoiced at the communication, and a few days afterward that exquisite cradle-song, "Schlummre und träume von künftiger Zeit," was expedited across the Channel to the lovely young mother and Mendelssohn's god-son, Felix Moscheles.

I have been furnished, both verbally and by letter, with many pleasing *traits* and details of Mendelssohn's life in Düsseldorf. The position he at that time assumed as an artist, and what he accomplished there as a director, we find related in the various biographies of Mendelssohn and Immermann; but his friends alone could tell of his private life. It is well known what delightful harmony subsisted from the commencement between the poet and the musician, and what hopes were excited for the stage from such a rare combination. Immermann was to conduct the Drama, and Mendelssohn the Opera. On the 28th of October, 1834, the Düsseldorf Theater opened with Kleist's "Prinzen von Homburg," and a "Festspiel," written for the occasion by Immermann. The crowded house was brilliant in the rich adornment of female beauty. Raphael's Parnassus was placed on the stage in the highest perfection by the painters, with a striking musical accompaniment composed by Mendelssohn. The gentle friend of the poet, Countess Ahlefeldt, whose delicate features and pensive expression were to be seen in a stage-box, listened in visible excitement to the poetry, her fair hand flinging on the stage, at the close, a laurel-wreath, the signal for a universal shower of flowers. The first opera performances under the direction of Mendelssohn were received with still greater enthusiasm—Mozart's "Don Juan," and Cherubini's "Wasserträger," and also Göthe's "Egmont," with Beethoven's music. These were flowers that had sprung to life from under a mass of rubbish, roses that had shot up in an uncultivated garden—giant power and giant energy such as a god-like enthusiasm for art could alone inspire, were requisite to unite in one harmonious whole all that lay scattered around. The community saw only the finished work, and rejoiced in it; no one knew how much patience, trouble, work, discord, and strife had preceded it. No doubt the very brilliant success of these operas, the powerful impression that music never fails to make on the public at large, the irresistible magic that it exercises above all on the people, caused Immermann to become uneasy about the fate of his dramatic representations, and induced him to make those unfortunate and much-discussed efforts to drive the opera at any cost into the background. Perhaps, also, the unconcealed endeavors of the fiery young master to secure the first place for his beloved art, caused the representative of "the irritable race of poets" to lose patience; at all events, there soon arose greater or lesser points of collision. Neither would yield a single hair's breadth, neither would move an inch from his place; and thus the estrangement of these two friends, once so intimate, every day increased, and, in spite of the daily intervention of others, quickly deepened into variance, and ended in a public breach of their connection. No decided opinion can be given on the subject of these complicated Düsseldorf conflicts, much less can they be discussed in detail; too many recent graves lie around on every side, on which the grass has not yet grown—who could have courage to invade those sacred resting-places!

And yet even in Düsseldorf, in spite of this disturbed atmosphere, and a sky alternately bright and overcast, that regal palm-tree, "St. Paul," calmly and surely waxed in growth.

A clever and congenial friend of Mendelssohn's, at that period a beautiful, young, and happy wife, and now a still young and happy grandmother, Malwine B. S——, speaks charmingly of the private life of Mendelssohn in those days, which formed such a welcome counterpoise to the chaos of unsatisfactory occupations, and the manifold annoyances of his artistic life there. Their first acquaintance began as follows :—

His parents and his sister Rebecca came to visit their beloved son and brother in his new home. They lived in the Breidenbach Hof, opposite the young married couple I have alluded to, a distinguished physician and his wife. Doubtless the bright eyes of the latter often glanced through the flowers in her window, at the happy family group opposite, of which the celebrated young music-director formed the center. One evening, after tea, when the young couple were sitting together, talking of their interesting *vis à vis*, rapid footsteps were heard on the stairs, and a hasty knock at the door, when Felix Mendelssohn rushed in, without his hat, in the greatest state of excitement, imploring the physician, in a few hurried words, to come with him instantly, as his mother had been suddenly taken ill. Dr. B—— at once hurried off with him to see the invalid. Frau Mendelssohn had been seized by a kind of apoplectic fit, and was unconscious, while the family were in the deepest distress by the side of their beloved mother. The necessary remedies were applied, and after watching with them through the night, the young doctor had the joy of being able to pronounce the precious patient out of danger.

Two days afterward, the old gentleman, with Felix and Rebecca, called to thank their new friend, and, with tears in their eyes, begged him and his wife to visit their much-loved and revered invalid the same afternoon. The young couple were only too delighted to accept this urgent invitation. When they entered the room they found the convalescent patient lying on a sofa; she welcomed her kind doctor and his charming companion with a bright smile. Beside her, exhausted by the fatigue and excitement of the previous days, lay Felix, asleep, his slender hand clasped in that of his mother, and his head resting on the corner of the sofa. The mother pointed to Felix with a beseeching glance, while holding out her other hand to greet her visitors. Her son was so sound asleep that he heard none of the little preliminaries attendant on a first introduction.

There he lay, his noble forehead bent down, his dark eyelashes resting on his cheeks, his well-cut lips gently closed, pale, and breathing softly—a most charming picture. Rebecca, a lovely young girl, in a paroxysm of overflowing spirits, so easily excited by the sense of danger escaped, could not withstand the temptation of sewing the skirts of the sleeper's coat to the sofa. Gently the mother, with eyes and lips, protested against this mischievous prank —but in vain; Rebecca persisted in her purpose. "Never can I forget," relates his friend, " the embarrassed yet laughing face of Felix when he awoke, and, on attempting to rise to welcome us, found that he was held fast. Those were memorable hours, which, both in their graver aspect and unconscious humor, caused a greater intimacy between us than months of the usual intercourse of social life. The conversation became forthwith as gay and lively as if among old friends. We were as frank and unconstrained as if we had known each other for years." So, in the course of conversation the young wife alluded, in a good-natured, laughing way, to some of the peculiarities of the Düsseldorf society. Felix started up with animation, and, stretching out his hand, laughing to the fascinating speaker, said, " All you say is true and just, and I think exactly as you do ; only, a pretty woman may venture to say so, whereas I must *not*—that is the difference!" Before leaving Düsseldorf, the Mendelssohns introduced their new friends to a family whose house they had looked upon as their most charming resource, and considered a place of rest, or a kind of home—the hospitable art-loving family of W——.

The family at that time consisted of the father, a stately mature man, though still in the prime of life, three sons, and two highly-gifted, amiable daughters. They were all musical ; the girls sang enchantingly ; and a finer tenor than that of Ferdinand, the eldest son, was perhaps never heard in Germany. The W—— house was a *rendezvous* for all artists far and near—a bright green oasis in the arid wilderness of the world, but a specially favorite resort of the Mendelssohn family—a station which you must stop at, and which Paul Mendelssohn very appropriately called "the grand rest."

Felix dedicated several books of songs to the sisters W——, and it was they who, unconsciously at that period, inspired his vocal compositions. How often did he arrive in their house with a newly-written MS. in his hand, a song for them, that they might sing it for him! One of those sweet, girlish voices would then render his musical ideas with clearness and warmth; what he had felt deeply thus assuming as it were a living form, and being as profoundly felt by the hearts of the singers, sounding afresh like an echo. The young composer would then start up in overflowing excitement, and seize the white hands of the singers, exclaiming, "This is joy of heart! It is thus that German songs ought to be sung!"

Those evenings in the society of the W—— family were Felix's greatest recreation and refreshment. When Ferdinand and the girls sang, Felix played with Rietz, the distinguished violoncello-player, or extemporized before this select circle so beautifully on themes he had just heard, that he enchanted every one, young and old. There, too, they played at forfeits, when Mendelssohn always seemed the merriest and most child-like of them all. Those who saw him flying about, dancing so gayly with young girls and married women, or with bandaged eyes guessing who touched him, and laughing amid all the confusion of merry voices, could scarcely realize that a few hours later this very same man—his thoughts as far removed from this mirthful scene as the heavens from the earth—his head bent over the text of "St. Paul," just received from his friend Pastor Schubring, was writing down those sublime melodies destined to flash through the world like rays of light. He often, too, came in the forenoon to the wife of the physician to try over some of his melodies, and to ask, playfully, "That sounds well; don't you think so?"

His friends, moreover, did not spoil him by praise; and he was by no means nurtured on the honeyed words of flattery. They were

much more disposed to criticize him unspar-
ingly, if he produced anything that one or another did not thoroughly approve of. How
often he sat among them, leaning his head on
his hands, with the written music before him,
saying, "But I really do think that I have in
this way best expressed my meaning; it stood
just so in my soul, and now I am so vexed that
you hear it differently; but still, I believe the
day will come when you will discover that I
was right—the hour will arrive when it will
sound better in your ears."

And the day infallibly came when they saw
it as he did. Hildebrandt remembers a saying
of Mendelssohn's, with regard to Father Haydn,
which I shall quote here as characteristic.

Once, on the occasion of a merry jovial meeting, a select circle of friends, with uplifted
glasses, found fault with the weakness of the
chorus in "The Seasons," in praise of wine.
"We should like to sing something far more
spirited in its place," said they, scornfully.
"The 'old Papa' must have been drinking
detestable wine at that time to put so little fire

into its praise." Mendelssohn smiled. "Father Haydn can well forgive your calumny," said he, "and can afford to wait patiently till you once more come to your senses. Let the frothy period of youth pass away, and then sing his chorus to a glass of wine, and tell me whether it still seems insipid. At this moment the wine itself is your chief object. When Haydn wrote that chorus, he did not drink wine as you do, merely to enjoy it, but only in order to gain strength for his work, and to rejoice in the strength it imparted. So I say again—Wait!"

"We often marveled," says Hildebrandt, "at all the wisdom in this young head. We constantly felt how immeasurably he was above us; and yet, at other times, he was as full of boyish mirth and high spirits as the youngest among us."

The enthusiasm is indescribable with which "St. Paul," even before its completion, was received, and studied in its separate parts, by the Düsseldorf circles. When Mendelssohn caused any of the choruses to be rehearsed, listeners assembled in crowds, and often burst forth into loud shouts of applause. The fair friend of Mendelssohn, to whom we have alluded, witnessed a most diverting interlude at one of these rehearsals. Mendelssohn requested Ferdinand von W——— to sing the recitative that, as usual, he brought with him just as he had written it down, and also the connecting passages in the "Chorus of the Heathens." The words in the text of these pages were certainly by no means distinctly written; and when the passage came, "When the heathens heard it, they were *glad*" (*froh*), it so happened that the glorious tenor voice sang with animation, "When the heathens heard it, they were *saucy*" (*frech*). This expression, so peculiarly Rhenish, in spite of the solemn mood of the audience, called forth an almost Homeric burst of laughter. The singer paused, a spasm contracted his face, and he looked across at Mendelssohn. He, however, was bending forward, both arms resting on the piano, convulsed with laughter. The singer now laughed also, and it was some time before either the director or any present were sufficiently composed to repeat or to listen to the treacherous passage in its original reading.

The first performance of " St. Paul," which subsequently took place at Düsseldorf, Mendelssohn directed himself, although at that time he belonged to Leipzig. His mother and his sisters and brother came from Berlin to attend it ; and, probably, never has this work been given to the ear in such perfection as on that occasion, during the first impetus of fervent enthusiasm for the composer and his creation. " St. Paul," indeed, had attained its full growth directly under the eyes of those who now took part in it. Each performer thought that he had a certain share in this wonderful production. One trifling passage alone did not go steadily ; one of the " false witnesses " made a mistake. Fanny Hensel, who was seated with the *contralti*, became as pale as death, bent forward, and, holding up the sheet of music, sang the right notes so steadily and firm that the culprit soon got right again. At the close of the performance, in the midst of all the jubilation, Felix tenderly clasped the hand of his helper in need, saying, with his sunny smile, " I am glad it was one of the *false* witnesses ! "

As at that epoch of Düsseldorf life, one art always stretched forth a helping hand to another; the Beethoven Sonatas also became, in a new form, a wondrous adornment of the various fêtes. Mendelssohn had harmonized several of these for instruments, and some of the movements were introduced with *tableaux vivants*, arranged in rare perfection, and, with the aid of beautiful female faces, and male heads full of character, produced the most brilliant effects. It formed a rare and harmonious combination of color, tone, and—men of genius. The " Funeral March," from the A major Sonata, has accompanied many to their final resting-place. Not till the autumn of the year 1836,—when that gifted young musician Robert Burgmüller was borne to his grave—did Mendelssohn compose a Funeral March himself, the effect of which was said to be very striking.

There was an attempt made, in a grander style and with the most careful preparations, to illustrate Händel's Oratorios in a similar manner; that is, to accompany their performance with *tableaux vivants*, and Mendelssohn was all fire and flame for this project. He relied on Händel's original idea of making his Oratorios effective on the masses by putting them on the stage with a certain degree of scenic splendor. Händel's "Israel in Egypt" was therefore at once produced with *tableaux vivants*. The most renowned artists painted the decorations; the surging sea and the noblest forms of Bible history met the eye in bright and living beauty. This representation produced a really overwhelming impression.

Many little incidents, recalled by friends, gleam like fitful rays of light respecting the artistic value of those days. One of Mendelssohn's favorite stories was an ancient Roman tradition of a motionless assembly of Senators, seated in death-like silence, whom a guileless Gaul mistook for stone statues, and was therefore bold enough to pluck the beard of one of

the circle, when the supposed statue started
into life and cut down the audacious Gaul with
his sword. In remembrance of this anecdote,
Mendelssohn and Hildebrandt agreed, that
whenever they met, no matter where, even in
the most aristocratic society, never to say "good
day" to each other without a certain form.
Hildebrandt was suddenly to stand still and
assume a stony face, when Mendelssohn was
to go up to him slowly and solemnly and pull
his beard, while he was in turn to submit to
a sharp Roman blow on the shoulder, which
dissolved the magic spell, and they were then
to greet each other with their usual cordiality.

In no place in the world could Mendelssohn
have found a warmer or more congenial soil
for the rapid development of his artistic nature
than in the Düsseldorf of that day. Would
this magic flower have bloomed as brightly if
grown on other ground? Surely continual
emulation, reciprocal influence, and cordial
intimacy with the most distinguished men,
must have acted like ripening rays of light.
But, as the mournful old song says:

> Bright as the sun may shine,
> It must decline at last;

and thus Mendelssohn's Düsseldorf life came to a close much earlier than was anticipated, by a summons to Leipzig as Director of the Gewandhaus Concerts.   Sebastian Bach's well-beloved " Lindenstadt " became the second home of his most fervent admirer.

CHAPTER III.

LEIPZIG.

On October 4, 1835, Felix Mendelssohn, amid the enthusiastic applause of a crowded audience, was directing in the hall of the venerable Gewandhaus, on the orchestra of which is inscribed the following maxim: "Res severa est verum gaudium." The programme consisted of that enchanting Overture, "Meeresstille und glückliche Fahrt;" Scene and Aria from "Lodoiska," by Cherubini, sung by the fine sympathetic voice of Fräulein Henriette Grabau; a violin Concerto by Spohr, played by his pupil, Music-Director Berka of Berlin; Introduction from Cherubini's "Ali Baba;" and finally, Beethoven's B-flat major Symphony.

With regard to Fräulein Grabau, Mendelssohn wrote to Hildebrandt—"I have here met with a singer who executes both Beethoven's songs and those of others so beautifully, that I am almost tempted to compose some new songs; but be tranquil, I am working busily at my ' St. Paul.' "

A fruitful musical autumn succeeded this charming commencement of Mendelssohn's first labors in Leipzig. Moscheles came over from England, and gave a brilliant concert, where he played with Mendelssohn his celebrated " Hommage à Händel," which, owing to this extraordinary combination of talent, was attended with the most unexampled success; and the much-admired tenor, Wild, melted every female heart by his rendering of the grand Belmont Aria in the " Seraglio."

The highly-gifted Chopin, during a short visit to Leipzig at that time, formed a friendship with Felix; the star of Klara Wieck, too, was then rising in the artistic firmament of Leipzig, and the tones of Ferdinand David's magic violin were heard for the first time in the Gewandhaus. Every effort was at once made to secure this dear friend of Mendels-

sohn's youth, and he was offered the situation
of Concertmeister of the Gewandhaus orchestra, vacant by the death of Mathäi. He accepted the offer, and is still to be seen at his
music-desk in Leipzig, one of the most brilliant centers of musical life there, and the soul
of the Conservatorium.

In the course of that autumn, Mendelssohn's
heart was saddened by his first severe sorrow; he lost his beloved father, to whom he
had always been, in his filial reverence, so
tenderly and lovingly submissive, which indeed his letters to his father, and also about
him, most touchingly prove. His letter to
Pastor Schubring, in Dessau, expresses his
deep affliction in a very affecting manner :—

"You have no doubt heard of the heavy
stroke that has fallen on my happy life, and
those dear to me. It is the greatest misfortune that could have befallen me, and a trial
that I must either strive to bear up against, or
must utterly sink under. I say this to myself
after the lapse of three weeks, without the
acute anguish of the first days, but I feel it

the more deeply; a new life must begin for me, or all must be at an end—the old life is now severed."

In another part of the letter he says:—

"I do not know whether you are aware that, more especially for some years past, my father was so good to me, so thoroughly my friend, that I was devoted to him with my whole soul, and during my long absence I scarcely ever passed an hour without thinking of him; but as you knew him in his own home with us, in all his kindliness, you can well realize my state of mind. The only thing that now remains is to do one's duty, and this I strive to accomplish with all my strength, for he would wish it to be so if he were still present, and I shall never cease to endeavor to gain his approval as I formerly did, though I can no longer enjoy it."

And this trial he bore bravely, taking refuge, with all the earnest purpose of his artistic soul, in a noble and grave work—the completion of his "St. Paul." Probably the chorus, "Behold! happy is he," sprang from the remembrance of the well-beloved and departed one, and doubtless many a tear fell on its pages.

According to my *own* feelings, nothing can denote more profound sorrow, and yet more resignation, piety, and sublimity, than this chorus. I do not think of what musicians say as to the beauty of the composition, it only seems to me that this "Behold!" must have strengthened and comforted the heart of the composer himself, and that of many others also. No one can hear it without tears; but the sorrow is that of a sufferer who has learned to say, "The Lord gave, and the Lord hath taken away; blessed be the name of the Lord!"

During the whole of the following winter, till far in the spring, he could not cast off the burden of his severe affliction, and his letters of that date are all written in the minor key. Thus he writes to the talented Orientalist, Friedrich Rosen, in London, too early snatched away by death :—

"I feel like a person waking drowsily. I cannot succeed in realizing the present, and there is a constant alternation of my old habitual cheerfulness and the most heartfelt deep grief, so that I cannot attain to anything like steady composure of mind. In the meantime, however, I occupy myself as much as possible, and that is the only thing that does me good. My position here is of the most agreeable nature—cordial people, a good orchestra, the most susceptible and grateful musical public; only just as much work to do as I like, and an opportunity of hearing my new compositions at once, which is, indeed, all I can wish. I have plenty of pleasant society besides, so that this would indeed seem to be all that was required to constitute happiness, were it not deeper seated!"

I may here make mention of a little three-fold relic that I lately saw, an admirably en-graved head of Göthe on a seal. Göthe himself gave the stone to Mendelssohn, and, in leaving England, Felix presented it to his dear friend Rosen, and now this gift of affection has passed into the hands of his brother Paul, as the last token of remembrance of the beloved departed, and cherished by him as a sacred treasure.

In the year 1835, besides completing his "St. Paul," Mendelssohn composed a Capriccio and Fugue for the piano, and likewise "Das Waldschloss," a song too little known, and which is imbued with the romance and fragrance of the forest.

All this grief was at last succeeded by a bright sunny day of joy—the performance of " St. Paul," to which I have already alluded, in Düsseldorf, with Fischer-Achten, Frau Bühnau-Grabau, and Mersing.

It was after this brilliant festival—Mendelssohn being at that time on a visit to Schadow—that a stranger was announced who wished to speak to him on a matter of importance. Presently there came into the charming salon, full of flowers, statues, and *chefs d'œuvre* of painting, a homely, quiet man, accompanied by a timid girl, scarcely beyond the age of childhood, her black hair hanging down in thick plaits on her shoulders, her large dark eyes glancing with nervous anxiety at the celebrated composer of " St. Paul," while the color on her cheeks varied from white to red. It was *Sophie Schloss*, afterward so renowned as a singer, and her father. The latter humbly entreated the master to give him his opinion about the voice of his child, requesting him to try it, as it depended solely on his verdict whether his little girl should be educated as a singer. Mendelssohn kindly stroked the head of the child, whose dark eyes met his encouraging glance. His few cheering words—and no one knew better how to speak thus, and to inspire self-reliance in genuine modesty—soon lit up the youthful face with a smile. "What will you sing to me?" "On the wings of song." "Really! Well, then, let us take flight together!" He seated himself at the piano, and looked once more at the little singer with a smile—and ah! who could smile like him, when wishing to inspire confidence in a timid heart?—and then the full tones of a grand contralto resounded in the large room. Sophie Schloss went fearlessly through her song; only just toward the close, the consciousness of her bold attempt, and the dread of her judge and his verdict, seemed all of a sudden to rush like a stream of lava on her remembrance, and the last tones were tremulous.

Mendelssohn's hands glided from the keys, and he said, " That was excellent! You have a voice of gold, and must positively become a great singer." And thus was the career of the young novice in art decided. Sophie Schloss took leave of the master, her face beaming with joy; the beautiful long tresses were now wound round her head, her short frocks lengthened, and a few weeks afterward the "little girl," with her portfolio under her arm, was to be seen in daily attendance at the Conservatoire in Paris, where she soon became Bordogni's favorite pupil, studying with unflagging energy and ardent zeal—"that I may soon be able to sing something tolerably good *to him*," said she, daily.

3*

CHAPTER IV.

Maiden fair!
Thy lustrous eyes
Shine brighter than the sun:
Beyond compare
The rarest prize
That manhood ever won.
Life and death alone with thee
Were joy to all eternity.

Blossoming flowers
Of endless hue
Before thy radiance die;
Through long, long hours,
Though tempests strew
The snow-flakes as they fly,
I watch, and linger at the goal,
For thee—thou idol of my soul!

MENDELSSOHN's stay in Leipzig was interrupted by a visit of some months to Frankfort-on-the-Maine, where he became the substitute of his invalid friend Schelble, who urgently required rest. I wonder whether any presentiment crossed his soul of the happiness that he was destined to find there, when he once more beheld that ancient city on the Maine, with its venerable dome and ancient watch-tower encompassed with a garland of blooming gardens and forest verdure, and adorned by the proud diadem of the Taunus? Whose heart would not beat more quickly at the sight of that enchanting spot, assuming at times a distinctly southern character, so glowing appears the coloring in the golden light of evening? And the susceptible, finely attuned soul of the artist, so alive to all the beauties of nature, received such impressions in double force.

From the date of the labors of the distinguished originator and director of the "St. Cecilia Association," Johann Nepomuk Schelble, a stirring musical life had reigned in Frankfort. Not only did they love music, but they advanced its interests in the most brilliant way in all its phases. Schelble's method of teaching singing, the results of which were so wonderful, produced numerous voices of rare beauty; he discovered and trained even children's voices, promoting their growth, just as a skillful gardener guards and cherishes his flowers, from the earliest seed to the developed blossom. The far-famed "St. Cecilia Association" consisted chiefly of the grateful pupils of this inimitable teacher.

At the time that Mendelssohn came to Frankfort, Schelble was both morally and physically broken down by bad health and trials of various kinds; thus the breath of a fresh breeze seemed to enter the hall when the youthful substitute of the sorrow-stricken master wielded his *bâton* for the first time to direct the vocal society. How many bright eyes and searching glances were eagerly directed toward him! how many fair lips were preparing to pronounce their verdict on him! He was of course already a celebrated man, a personage of renown; indeed Mendelssohn himself wrote on this subject, in his playful way: " The ' Melusina ' and the ' Hebrides ' are as familiar to them as to us at home (I mean No. 3 Leipziger Strasse)." But the city on the Maine had invariably shown great self-reliance in musical matters. It did not rush like many into a display of enthusiasm, because others had set the example, but paused till the feeling was no longer to be resisted.

How youthful and delicate was the aspect of the new director! How slender and elegant his figure! his demeanor rather careless, his movements animated and graceful. He advanced to the piano, and made a short speech; as he playfully writes to his family, "I made a speech that deserves to have been written down."

Any one who ever heard Mendelssohn speak extempore, could certainly never forget it; there was something quite irresistible in his mode of address, which was intelligent and natural, peculiarly natural—no striving after effect, no fine phrases, but thoroughly cordial and amiable. The tone of his voice, too, captivated all hearts; his animated countenance, his matchless smile, the flash of his eye, and a slight occasional gesture of the hand. When he spoke thus, every one gladly did what he wished, and saw everything in the light he desired, even though a short time previously they had solemnly vowed neither to do nor to see as he did. He was quite victorious in the "St. Cecilia Association;" they were not only

secretly enchanted with him, but spoke enthusiastically of him in public—an occurrence
more rare in Frankfort than in any city whatever.

The first evening that Mendelssohn directed,
he selected choruses from " Samson " to be
sung, and portions of Bach's B minor Mass.
" Bach went almost faultlessly," writes he,
" and I had a fresh opportunity of admiring
how Schelble, by dint of his admirable tena-
city, has succeeded in making his will obeyed."

Mendelssohn's social life assumed a most
agreeable form; he was sought after and
courted in every way; the first families in
Frankfort vied with each other in giving
him fêtes.   The chance presence of his
friend Hiller was a source of particular satisfaction to him, he having likewise felt an impulse, when in a " fair and distant land," to
re-visit his beloved native city.   Doubtless
many a pleasant hour flitted by in that well-
known corner room, whence there was a view
of the ancient Wartthurm, and where much
good music was heard; there, too, many a

critical verdict was passed, not only on music, but—on the fair ladies of Frankfort, to whom Frau Hiller, so good a judge of her sex, and so justly proud of her countrywomen, directed the attention of her gifted friend. Many musical birds of passage migrated thither at that time, Rossini among others—that ever-youthful, gay, dazzling, witty man of the world; there was always some fresh excitement and work "for hands and hearts in plenty," as the "Müllerlied" says. In such society, and in such sunshine, the veil of sorrow cast by the death of the father on the heart of the son, was gradually withdrawn, the sky over his head once more became blue and clear, and roses bloomed again on the earth. "All seemed beautiful and bright around," he writes, "such fruitfulness, richness of verdure, gardens, and fields, and the beautiful blue hills as a background; and then a forest beyond; to ramble there in the evenings under the splendid beech-trees, among the innumerable herbs and flowers, and blackberries and strawberries, makes the heart swell with gratitude." With regard to his own labors—that is, compositions—much does not seem to have been accomplished during this happy season. Mendelssohn's stay in Frankfort was in reality a *dolce far niente*, with the exception of his occupation in the " St. Cecilia Association." Direct intercourse with nature, and with a few chosen friends, was for him the very highest enjoyment; he never cared for brilliant society, nor for rushing from fête to fête. The esteemed musician had received from an agreeable Frankforter, whose acquaintance he made in Leipzig, a letter of introduction to the widow of Consistorialrath Jeanrenaud, the venerated Pastor of the French Protestant church ; and here it was that the destiny of his heart was decided. In that very house Mendelssohn met with those sweet eyes, " blue and loving," that were one day to become the light of his life. The time came at last when he could sing these lines :—

> There is a child with a rosy mouth,
> And bright brown curling hair;
> In east or west, in north or south,
> None with her can compare.

Cécile Jeanrenaud, whose mother belonged to a distinguished emigrant family, was at that period considered one of the most beautiful girls in Frankfort, always so rich in female charms, where indeed to this day, as in Saxony, "fair maidens grow on every tree;" and when I now recall her image as I first saw her, though some time after her marriage, I feel that to this present hour she has always remained my *beau idéal* of womanly fascination and loveliness. I admired her with all the impetuosity of a young imaginative creature. Her figure was slight, of middle hight, and rather drooping, like a flower heavy with dew, her luxuriant golden-brown hair fell in rich curls on her shoulders, her complexion was of transparent delicacy, her smile charming, and she had the most bewitching deep blue eyes I ever beheld, with dark eyelashes and eyebrows. Such was the fair wife of Mendelssohn. How often, amid "snow-flakes as they fly," have I stood in a corner of the Gewandhaus stairs, waiting to see her glide past me at the close of the concert, when her fair face looked forth through the transparent vail in which it was wrapped, like the bright moon emerging from dark clouds, while her eyes shone like stars.

I was once in her room, when she addressed a few friendly words to me. A singer with whom I was acquainted had brought me with her, and while the two ladies were conversing, I gazed at Cécile Mendelssohn in silent admiration. Ah! such a feeling of enthusiasm, known to few, is, after all, the most delightful thing in the world! To be able to admire the grand or the beautiful as I have a thousand times done, and still do, is a blessed frame of mind—perhaps somewhat akin to the ecstacy produced by the intoxication of opium, but without the depressing effects it leaves. On that day Cécile Mendelssohn wore a dark-blue silk dress, a lace collar and cuffs, without ornament; but her whole aspect had a *Madonna* air—the only way in which I can define it— what Berthold Auerbach so beautifully calls *Marienhaft.* The celebrated Magnus, in Berlin, subsequently painted her. I never saw the portrait, which was much praised, but I only wish I could have painted her as I saw her on that day. Her manner was generally thought too reserved; indeed she was considered cold, and called "the fair Mimosa." In music we have an expressive term, "calm but impassioned," and this I deem an appropriate inscription for the portrait of Cécile Mendelssohn. The two sisters, Cécile and Julie Jeanremaud, formed a charming contrast. The one brilliant and gay, playful, fragile as a vapor, fairy-like, with fair hair, and eyes as blue as forget-me-nots; while the other was grave, with that wonderful expression in her glance that realized the tradition of "eyes of consolation."

Felix Mendelssohn then wooed this youthful virgin rose with

> Yearning,
> And burning,
> In passion and pain,*

like every other mortal in a similar condition.

> Thy lustrous eyes shine brighter than the sun,

many a day and many a night found its echo in his heart, and that he never failed to lie in wait for her is also indubitable, and even *he*

---

* From the Translation of "Egmo..t" by A. D. Coleridge, Esq.

was forced sometimes to " wait long, long hours " before she appeared—though, let us hope, not as in the song, " when tempests strew the snow-flakes as they fly," for it chanced to be the lovely spring and summer time.

But assuredly no effort was irksome to him for her sake; while all his anxiety, waiting, and watching were speedily swept away and forgotten when at last he saw her, " the idol of his soul."

The state of excitement and agitation caused by such mental emotions in the delicately organized nature of Mendelssohn, subjected to all those alternations of "rapturous delight" and " deadly sorrow," is best proved by the advice of his clever young physician, Dr. Spiess, in Frankfort, who sent off the young Director of the " St. Cecilia Association " with all speed to Schevening, in order to strengthen his nerves; and his betrothal did not take place till after his return from those sea-baths.

A gay rural excursion had been arranged— a *réunion* of agreeable people, quite an *embarras de richesses* of lovely women; while jests and laughter resounded everywhere in the glorious sunshine. An expedition to the beautiful Taunus had been fixed on, and in that charming spot, Kronthal, words were at length spoken that eyes had long since betrayed ; and a happy engaged couple emerged from the green forest, and were greeted by the most cordial congratulations—and it was thus the musician found his earthly St. Cecilia. When Mendelssohn returned to Leipzig, the most ardent and loving aspirations were wafted thence to his beloved bride, and that wonderfully touching

> Ah ! western winds, I envy thee
> Thy moist and balmy breath.

The sun of love now matured flowers of song in richest luxuriance, and the book (Op. 34) that Mendelssohn dedicated to his fair sister-in-law is imbued with a profound happy love and the rejoicing of an overflowing heart, not to be found in any of his other works.

We find a blank in Mendelssohn's published letters; we have the singing and ringing tones of this most joyful period of his life, but not one *written* word ; not in the whole of that rich treasury do we gather the slightest indication of the all-important relations to his bride and his wife. In reply to a remark of mine on this subject, a dear and valued friend said: "Many of those who were eye-witnesses of Mendelssohn's domestic felicity have deeply lamented that all allusions to it should have been omitted; but this was prompted by the wish to respect the will of her who is now no more, and who was always so averse to such publicity: these feelings induced her, during her last illness, and with a presentiment of approaching death, to burn, with her own hands, every letter addressed to herself by her husband. Strange as this proceeding may appear to many, we, who were near and dear to her, are too well acquainted with her reasons to trench on sensibilities which have long since remingled in the great All of love eternal."

How many charming pages, greetings from heart to heart, must at that period have flown between Leipzig and Frankfort!—and when I hear the Göthe-Mendelssohn song, "Die Liebende schreibt," I always think of the blue eyes of the girl, thoughtfully dwelling on the page, her luxuriant curls drooping, and her cheeks flushing like one softly saying to her lover:—

> Afar from friends, afar from thee,
> I can but think of all that's dear;
> But aye with thought comes memory,
> And with remembrance comes a tear.

During the sunny times of 1836, '37 and '38, were written the splendid 42nd Psalm, the D minor Quartette for stringed instruments, a pianoforte concerto, several quartettes, preludes, and fugues for piano and organ, a serenade for pianoforte and orchestra, a sonata, a quartette for male voices, and the enchanting song "Im Grünen" for soprano, alto, tenor, and bass, a "Song without words," in A minor, and an exquisite Book of Songs, containing "Suleika," the 95th Psalm, and also springing with such fervor from the depths of the heart, "O come, let us sing unto the Lord." Leipzig felt the warmest sympathy in the happiness of its favorite. Both in private society and in the public concert-hall, his betrothal was celebrated. In the Gewandhaus concert, at the following words in the final chorus of "Fidelio," "He who has gained a charming wife," a loud shout of rejoicing burst forth, on which Mendelssohn, excited by the emotions of the moment and by his own feelings, seated himself at the piano, and extemporized for the first time before an assembled public. He took up the theme in question from "Fidelio," and varied it in such a rich, diversified, and astonishing manner, that all the audience were profoundly touched. Whole volumes of letters and poems seemed to lie in these tones and chords, hurrying as it were " on the wings of song," over hills and dales and valleys to the far-distant beloved one.

The most important musical incident of that date was the performance of " St: Paul." Mendelssohn conducted the rehearsals with un wearied zeal; and the orchestra, as well as the singers, 300 in number, practiced and studied the work with the most intense good-will and delight. The performance itself, in the illu- minated Pauline Church, had a most glorious effect. The greatest excitement prevailed in the whole town, and, for once, critics were exceptionally unanimous in their admiration of the work, and of the manner in which it was performed. There was not a single person present who did not heartily and cordially bestow on the young composer the fresh laurel-wreath, entwined by fair hands, and laid on this director's desk. Then came the "merry month of May," and with it Mendelssohn's wedding-day.

Felix and Cécile were married in the Wallon Church at Frankfort, in the presence of a congregation among whom their pastor, the father of the lovely bride, had so successfully labored. All Frankfort was astir on that day to see the young couple. After the wedding was over, the happy pair took refuge from the world in the romantic depths of the Black Forest, dreaming away days such as are rarely vouchsafed to mortals. Rinaldo lay at Armida's feet, only with the difference that this Rinaldo never, like the hero of Gluck, asked, "Armida, why dost thou flee from me?"

Düsseldorf was the object of their first ex-

4

cursion. Mendelssohn brought his young wife to his dear old friends there. It was Höllenbart (Hildebrandt), in fact, who often jestingly advised Felix, when, by his nervous restlessness, he disturbed his companions and tore his white handkerchief with his teeth, to take to smoking in order to tranquilize him — or to take a wife. " Have I not shown good sense in preferring to take such a wife as this ? " he said, with a happy smile, when they met again.

The fair friend of Mendelssohn, to whom I have already alluded, described a charming evening with the W—— family during his stay on that occasion. The old father of the family was then in Berlin with his daughters, so the son, Ferdinand, begged Frau Malwine to do the honors of the house for him. How joyfully she acceded to this! Frau Jeanrenaud and her eldest daughter had accompanied the young couple ; Graf Nasselrode with his wife and beautiful daughter were present ; Rietz, Mendelssohn's worthy successor, the Schadows, Stienbrücks, and others. The most unaffected gayety pervaded the little circle; Mendelssohn was in the most brilliant spirits; and the Madonna face of Cécile, the queen rose among all the lovely women present, excited universal enthusiasm. After supper there was music. While Mendelssohn was playing Beethoven's "Kreutzer Sonata" with Rietz, and all were reverentially listening, a little mouse glided out of a corner and sat in the midst of the circle motionless, as if spell-bound by the magic tones. No doubt it would have remained in the same position till the playing ceased, had not one of the ladies made an abrupt gesture in horror of the formidable monster, which caused a slight commotion, and drove away the four-footed enthusiastic amateur.

During this visit to Düsseldorf, a splendid edition of "St. Paul" was presented to Mendelssohn, embellished by the finest compositions of the Düsseldorf painters. Schrödter composed the title-page. The noble modesty of Felix's nature, notwithstanding all his artistic self-consciousness, was here again most pleasingly displayed. "I could not show this to any one without feeling ashamed," said he. On which Cécile came forward, and, placing her hand on the work, looked at her husband with beaming eyes, saying, "Then give it to me; I will show it to every one with pride and joy."

All who came into familiar contact with Mendelssohn were well acquainted with his modesty; his mother used to call him "the reverse of a charlatan;" but Frau Malwine S—— still remembers a speech of Paul Mendelssohn's with regard to this peculiarity in his brother's character. At a supper-party, given after one of the Düsseldorf musical festivals to the composer of "St. Paul," a fair lady present requested the brother of the celebrated director to give his health. His answer, however, was very decided. "I dare not do so; Felix would take it so terribly amiss on my part—not one of his family would run such a risk."

During his whole life, Düsseldorf was ever and always a favorite resting-place of Felix

Mendelssohn's. It was there also where he first learned to know and to love the veteran master Spohr. He returned thither as often as he could, and his friends there saw first of all many of his most important creations, while beloved and familiar voices sang for him, in a small select circle, many an *opus* of which the world had as yet no presentiment, and he also played to them what no ear had previously heard. With what rejoicing, with what enthusiasm was he ever welcomed there, by the public as well as in the houses of his friends! When he came, it seemed always like one grand family festival, the whole town taking an interest in his arrival, and looking on him as a kind of property of their own, and sunning themselves in the brightness of his fame.

The Whitsuntide Festival of 1839, directed by Mendelssohn, with Julius Rietz, may be pronounced one of the most brilliant epochs in the musical annals of Düsseldorf. Händel's "Messiah" was performed, and Beethoven's Mass in C, and likewise, for the first time, that splendid work of Mendelssohn's, the 42nd

Psalm. A triad of female singers was there united, such as could be rarely met with in similar perfection. The fair-haired Auguste von Fassmann, the most aristocratic "Countess" in Mozart's "Figaro" that ever sang the lament of "Dove sono;" the enchanting Clara Novello, whose voice was as fresh and redolent of spring as her face and her disposition; and the nightingale of contraltos, Sophie Schloss.

During the rehearsal, when Sophie Schloss had sung her first recitative, Mendelssohn suddenly laid down his *bâton*, and bending forward over his desk to the singer, he asked with amusing gravity, "Tell me once more—is it really the same little girl with long black plaits of hair who has just sung so admirably?"

Clara Novello on that day sang like a harbinger of spring, or a glad exulting lark, while nothing could be more deeply impressive than the faith and fervent belief of her rendering of the air, "I know that my Redeemer liveth."

She appeared on that occasion for the first time on the Rhine, though already renowned in England as its most favorite singer. The musical notices of that concert season, on the subject of the fascinating songstress, recall the triumphal career of a Sontag. The pure silvery ring of her voice, the thorough cultivation of her organ, her finished shake and brilliant execution, excited the greatest admiration. Mendelssohn had already heard Clara Novello at the Birmingham Musical Festival, which he directed soon after his marriage, while Cécile remained with her mother and sister; he had invited the charming vocalist to come to Leipzig, where she sang in the Gewandhaus amid the most lively enthusiasm. This star also, like many another in the musical horizon, is now set. Clara Novello is become a lady of aristocracy, and has long since retired from public life.

With what delight Sophie Schloss-Guhrau, in a letter now lying before me, speaks of those former days in Düsseldorf! With what warmth she recalls her celebrated colleagues, and their amiability toward her, a youthful *débutante :* the beaming kindness of Mendelssohn after the performance of the Beethoven Mass, " which went so splendidly, that it was quite a pleasure to hear it!" She refers with peculiar delight to the third day of the Festival, when Mendelssohn played his D minor Concerto with an unprecedented storm of applause, and accompanied so many songs on the pianoforte; and the joyous supper, where the distinguished master sat between M'me Fassmann and Clara Novello, and little Sophie Schloss opposite, who, in spite of the marble vases filled with fragrant flowers, contrived again and again to steal secret glances of admiration at the master, whose countenance seemed lit up with joy; his eyes beamed, jest and earnest alternated on his lips. M'me Fassmann bent graciously toward him, her long fair curls almost touching his hands; while Clara Novello pouted, burying her sweet face in a large nosegay of flowers, playing so prettily her part of jealousy, when he talked once rather longer to his right-hand neighbor; amusing herself, too, by pelting her little colleague *vis à vis* with flower-leaves; the little colleague herself looking quite grave, and thinking in her own mind how pleasant it must be to sit thus wholly *sans gêne* beside the composer of "St. Paul," and to talk to him, and people like him. On that evening she little anticipated how soon and how often this would be her own case.

At the close of this musical festival, Mendelssohn engaged M'lle Schloss for the Leipzig concerts in the ensuing winter.

It was at one of these rehearsals of the "Messiah," that Mendelssohn started up from the piano in the most violent agitation, exclaiming in terror, "I am deaf!" His friendly physician was instantly sent for, and the attack soon passed away; but Cécile used afterward to tell with a smile how conscientiously, day and night, the patient swallowed the little powder prescribed by his beloved medical attendant.

I was also told of another incident that occurred during one of those musical times at Düsseldorf, which bears witness to the marvelous ear and memory of Mendelssohn.

At one of these festivals, the Pastoral Symphony was to be performed on the second day. Mendelssohn had come straight from England, just in time to direct the rehearsal. When the orchestra were assembled, and Mendelssohn proceeded to his desk, by some inconceivable negligence, the score of the Symphony was not forthcoming, nor was there one to be found at the moment in Düsseldorf. " Let us begin, gentlemen," said Mendelssohn, in a peremptory tone ; " I think I shall be able to direct the first part from memory." So, raising his magic *báton*, the orchestra began. It seemed then as if that wonderful work had actually been the creation of his own spirit, the child of his own soul. Every tone was in his heart and in his ears, every separate part in his memory. Amid all the crashing and sounding of instruments, not a single hesitation, or unsteady note, nor, in fact, the most trifling defect, escaped his notice. He darted about between his desk and the various instruments, and his ardor was so kindled that he directed the whole Symphony without a check, from beginning to end, by heart. The orchestra were quite enraptured, and they gave him an enthusiastic flourish of trumpets, and from that moment there was no

musician that did not swear by his name. His
memory, according to the testimony of all his
friends, was almost fabulous. What he once
heard, he *never* forgot ; and if years afterward
any piece of music was discussed that had ever
met his ear, he invariably knew it by heart.*

It was the same wonderful artist and renowned composer who, during the long intervals of the performance, contrived dexterously
to withdraw from all ovations—to rest and
cool. One glance sufficed to summon his friend
Hildebrandt to his side, when both slipped
away together, through a side-door, and walked
off to Hildebrandt's house, close to the Becker
Music Hall, where, quickly divesting themselves of their coats and boots, and casting
themselves on the green turf of the shady

---

* The translator can bear witness to Mendelssohn's extraordinary
memory. At a small Court concert in Dresden, at the close of 1846,
the King of Saxony requested her to name a theme on which Mendelssohn might extemporize. She named Gluck's "Iphigenie,"
which had been given on the previous evening at the Opera. The
King mentioned to Mendelssohn the theme selected, on which he
said: "Your Majesty, till last night I have not heard that Opera
for seven years, but I comply with your Majesty's commands.'"
He extemporized in the most surprising manner, not omitting one
of the most important airs in that grand Opera—a wonderful *tour
de force*.

little garden, they were supplied by the kind hostess with refreshing beverages. There they lay on the grass, their arms crossed under their heads, looking up at the sky, quite silent and quite happy. A short time after thus "bleaching," the elegant director was again to be seen, in a black coat and white neck-cloth, in his place at the director's desk, with his usual grave demeanor, being now once more the Kapellmeister, Felix Mendelssohn-Bartholdy.

An amusing introduction of Lindblad to Hildebrandt took place in the confusion of one of these festivals. Mendelssohn was seen making his way through the crowd toward his friend, followed by a fine-looking man, whose blue eyes looked round inquisitively. Felix seized Hildebrandt's hand, saying, "See, here is Lindblad, who wrote those charming songs! Lindblad, see! This is the man who painted ' The Sons of Edward ;' " and the next moment he disappeared in the crowd.

Long, long afterward—many a grief had since then burdened his soul, and from many a dear friend had he been for ever severed—Mendelssohn revisited his beloved friends in Düsseldorf, bringing with him his wife and child. Frau Malwine S—— met him on the threshold of her hospitable house, but was forced to beg him not to enter it, as two of her children were laid up with measles; so they all proceeded to W——. After supper, Mendelssohn seated himself, as formerly, at the piano, and took his little son Karl on his knee. At first he played in subdued tones, as if in a dream, while the child sat motionless, his eyes fixed on his father's hands. He then gently put him down, though the handsome boy continued to stand beside him, and Mendelssohn played on and on, every moment more beautifully, more touchingly, until all those around were in tears; and when he ceased, sighs and low sobs alone betrayed the overwhelming impression he had made. Then Cécile rose, and going up to him softly, she seized the hand that was hanging down, kissed it, and gently retreated. He raised his eyes to hers—it was a wonderful look; well might she esteem herself happy to whom it was directed!

CHAPTER V.

My own Leipzig concert recollections date
from the first appearance of the charming
Rhinelander Sophie Schloss—the recollections
of a girl scarcely emerged from childhood, but
a musical enthusiast! Of course, whatever our
names might be, we were all devoted to Mendelssohn. How distinctly I remember a day,
when I had just come home from school, and
was with my dear father on the Promenade
(that celebrated promenade, always so frequented between twelve and one o'clock), when
he said, " Look ! here come Mendelssohn and
his wife ! " I also remember that I would
gladly have done homage to him as a king, and
that, as he drew near, I could not make up my
mind whether to look at him or at her as they
advanced, and finally fixed my eyes on him,
while he greeted my father kindly. Of Cécile
Mendelssohn I had only the fleeting impression

of wonderful hair and blue eyes, beaming from under a dark velvet bonnet; but a finished picture of him and his grandly-modeled head was at once impressed upon my memory. He wore what was then called a Spanish cloak, that entirely concealed his figure. I have never hitherto seen any portrait (the one by Hildebrandt I have unfortunately never met with) that represents that artistic head as it lives in my memory; there is something effeminate and sentimental in all the Mendelssohn portraits, which were certainly not the attributes of the living head. A marvelously executed little ivory *relief*, a profile in the possession of a musical friend of the deceased master, Knaur's statuette, and the large bust, alone are exempt from this character, and therefore bear more affinity to the image in my memory. His hair was black and curling, the forehead of the highest order of intellectual beauty, the nose somewhat bent, the lips well chiseled, the shape of the face oval, the eyes irresistible, brilliant, and spiritual. His slender figure, scarcely attaining to middle size, seemed to increase in hight and to become imposing when he stood at his director's desk.   His hands were of remarkable beauty; Carus, that connoisseur of human beings and hands, would have defined them as " full of soul."   A very graceful movement of the head was peculiar to him; and when he carelessly threw it back, while his rapid glance, like that of a general, passed in array his musical forces, there was not one among them who did not at that moment silently vow to do his duty to the uttermost.   He appeared elegant and calm while directing; no peculiarities attracted the attention of the audience; not a vestige of embarrassment, and yet entire security.

No words can tell the devotion with which the different members of the orchestra clung to him.   But then how careful he was of them, how warmly he had their interests at heart, what an open ear and open hand he had for all their complaints!   He was not satisfied with the temporary addition to their salary of the 500 dollars that he had wrung out of the magistrates for their benefit; he never rested till he succeeded in effecting a real improvement in the position of the members of the orchestra.

"Just because the orchestra is not an article of luxury, but the most necessary and important basis for a theater—just because the public invariably regard with more interest articles of luxury than more essential things—on this very account, it is a positive duty to endeavor to effect, that what is legitimate and necessary should not be disparaged and superseded by a love of glitter."

Such noble, unselfish energy, shunning neither trouble nor efforts, could not fail in obtaining shortly a proportionately noble result. Mendelssohn succeeded in getting the considerable legacy of an art-loving burgher applied to founding a school for music, and afterward devoted his full powers to this young institution, which, in spite of the gloomy prophecies of many a misanthrope, soon sprung up fresh and vigorous. In fact, the whole of the musical life in Leipzig was in his hands. Thus, by degrees, all was ordered and arranged according to Mendelssohn's wish

4

and will, and for the general weal and welfare.

In those days there were three representatives of an earlier period who must have particularly attracted the attention of the youthful Kapellmeister—the two founders of the once celebrated "Cecilia," a musical paper, Hofrath Rochlitz and Gottlob Wilhelm Fink, and the ex-director of the Gewandhaus concerts, August Pohlenz. How vividly I can see him before me at this moment—my first singing-master, the good and highly esteemed music-director Pohlenz, the composer of so many charming quartettes, so many pleasing songs, the instructor of so many celebrated singers, and who had also trained the silvery voice of his own wife. He was a cheerful, original man, whom we all deeply lamented when he was suddenly taken from us and borne to his last resting-place. Who could ever forget that droll solid figure with all its vivacity, the quaint face and small eyes hidden by huge spectacles, the inimitable tone of his voice when he sang us over any passage, the nimbleness of his thick fingers when accompanying the warm, faithful heart and the musical soul that dwelt within that homely exterior? A great deal has been said about the mortifications Pohlenz underwent by the appointment of Mendelssohn; indeed, even his sudden death on March 10th, 1842, was ascribed to the neglect and irritation he had been subjected to. These assertions, however, like many others with regard to the musical life of that period, belong entirely to the realm of the imagination. Although benevolence formed the basis of Mendelssohn's nature, and few understood as he did how to honor and draw forth those who were still in darkness, he had a high opinion of Pohlenz as a teacher of singing, while he valued him no less as a musician, and lost no opportunity of expressing this to all who were disposed to listen.

Mendelssohn was, indeed, a genuine child of his time, in the fullest sense of the word; he brought about the transition from classical to modern music; in his oratorios he "sang a new song unto the Lord." He felt that, as all faith must be based on Holy Writ, so this new music must be founded on tradition, and frequently gave it as his opinion that all our knowledge and working must have their roots in the past. He wrote to Hildebrandt from Leipzig, with regard to an old musician, as follows: "The man's appearance touched me because it belonged to the past, just as a queue or a peruke never seemed ridiculous in my eyes, but rather something sad and solemn." With such sentiments as these, he certainly never could have looked askance at an honest, old-fashioned colleague. There were similar reports about Mendelssohn's relations to Schumann, which, however, afterwards received the most triumphant refutation from the admiration and delight with which he played Schumann's works, recommending them for performance, and also himself accompanying Schumann's songs. Any one who could conceive this soaring artistic soul capable of so base a feeling as that of envy, must have been utterly and wholly deficient in the power of comprehending a noble and high-souled nature.

Wilhelm Fink, the clever musical critic and editor of the "Musikalischen Haus-Schatz," once a celebrated preacher, and an amiable man, was the center of a small circle who formed a sort of passive opposition to the new director. This opposition, however, proceeded not so much from Fink himself as from his second wife, a highly cultivated pupil of John Field, who, by the advent of Mendelssohn, found the pleasing talent of her second daughter, Charlotte, thrown into the shade. Her disinclination to come in any way into contact with Mendelssohn was hightened when the hand of death was laid on the head of the young girl, on whom so many hopes rested, and this feeling was only extinguished with the life of the sorely-bereaved mother. Wilhelm Fink was the first to follow his child to the grave, tenderly nursed and deeply mourned by his attached and loving daughters; his wife, although a severe sufferer, survived him some years. How often we brought flowers into her quiet sick chamber, when she made us tell her of the outside world, and, in return, talked to us of the far richer world within, as she used to call it. She would then share with us those relics of the past stored up in her memory, when her stern face became animated and glowing, and her eyes lost their gloom as she spoke of her life in Russia, of her renowned instructor, and of Ludwig Berger and his fair-haired German wife, who died of home-sickness in brilliant Petersburg, and also about the handsome Emperor Alexander.

Hofrath Rochlitz was one of those pleasing old men who recall a clear, bright autumn day. He had passed a stirring and prolific life; his sun was gradually sinking, but he looked forward to its setting with the cheerful serenity of a sage. His speaking eyes, his talent for conversation, his Jean Paul humor, and his youthful enthusiasm for all that was beautiful in art and nature, in what shape soever he met with it, made him exceedingly attractive. The most charming relations subsisted between him and Mendelssohn, and there was something irresistible in the manner in which the young revered artist persisted in making himself subordinate to age and merit, while, on the other hand, no one could respond to this homage more amiably than Rochlitz.

Many youthful "people of mark" of that day emerge from the mists of memory. The lovely Luise Schlegl Köster, with her fair curls, a pupil of our Pohlenz, whom he always held up to us as a pattern, and whose splendid voice I still seem to hear singing Mozart's "Davidde Penitente" in the Pauliner Kirche. When the high C rang through every corner of the dusky church, my dear father, whose heart beat so warmly for music, at the close of the performance went up to the singer in his delight, and said some fervent words of praise, while I stood in silence by his side, looking at the singer and gazing with the utmost admiration at her delicate features and golden hair, quite ready now to admit that Pohlenz was justified in saying, " Luise will go ten times further than you will ever do; not at all on account of her glorious voice, but because she works like a trumpeter, and you do not."

I also remember the appearance of Elisa

Merti, an elegant young Belgian, so graceful in her movements, who sang such lovely French Romances and florid Ariettes in the Gewandhaus. A lively set of young people formed at that time a critical concert audience, the members of one of the gayest little musical circles in the world, who all gave each other *rendez-vous* at the Gewandhaus concerts, on those far-famed Thursday evenings. Many many looked down on us at that time, shaking their heads in disapproval of such " fledglings" presuming to usurp the places of those who were highly cultivated; and yet it was not from the midst of the " fledglings" that, during a sudden pause in a Beethoven Symphony, the words " bacon paste," the subject of conversation between two ladies, sounded distinctly through that hall, the motto of which is " Res severa est verum gaudium." Oh, bright and memorable musical garland ! how has it since been scattered by every wind. And yet we then thought that it would for ever remain the same !

I believe that Mendelssohn, who knew nothing whatever of our doings, would, like every warm-hearted musician, have been pleased to see how much we were *in earnest* in our studies. What we accomplished was as incomplete as most juvenile productions, but enthusiasm for music was deep and fervent within each of us. Then there was such happiness in being able to sing and play together; we took such harmless pleasure in the weak tea, herring salad, and mulled wine, and in all our little innocent interests and passions—and likewise in Schubert and Beethoven, Mozart and Haydn, Father Bach and Mendelssohn. How they rise before me, all those charming girlish heads, fair and dark, and those bright eyes, many of which since then have been " too used to weep," and those youthful cavaliers, who have long ago won names in different ways, and have long enjoyed titles and orders! How thoroughly were we in earnest in what we attempted, and carefully studied after our own fashion ; how we mutually sat in judgment on each other, and dreaded each other ; and how we all unanimously agreed in our enthusiasm for the one person who was the chief interest in Leip-

zig—Felix Mendelssohn! How many times
in the course of those evenings we drank his
health, how many fair lips gave· toasts in his
honor, while bright eyes sparkled at the words!
We had also our particular favorites in the
Gewandhaus concerts, and many a celebrity
failed in winning our approbation; whereas
we were sometimes loud in praise of those
who did not till much later in life justify our
enthusiasm.   With what interest did we observe and discuss every gesture of the most
distinguished members of the orchestra; above
all, how closely we watched any exchange of
smiles or glances between David and Mendelssohn, and the friendly nod or frown of Klin-
gel!   It was then, and still is a singular arrangement of the Gewandhaus Hall, that the
greater part of the audience do not sit opposite the orchestra, but face each other; thus
we had to twist our necks awry the whole
time, till we were exhausted, in order to see
Mendelssohn directing. Sometimes, during the
long ·interval, he was to be seen in one of the
two boxes above the orchestra, chatting for a

time. I think a Gewandhaus concert seen in perspective from the boxes on a level with the chandelier, must have given the impression of a bed of flowers, in the rich adornment of those pretty heads, dark and fair and gayly decked, and all those elegant *toilettes* where brilliant colors preponderated; and though there was much to hear, assuredly there was not less to see. Alas! how many a fragrant rose, then in its bloom, has long been faded and dead! I seem to see vividly before me the much-admired and beloved Isidore P——, afterwards Frau von G——, with her wonderful gazelle eyes, her dazzling complexion and dark hair, always dressed in vapory white, as if in a transparent vail. I see the lovely sisters Celeste and Lisbeth K——, in all their grace and charm, the delicate P——, the *piquante* Marie B——, and many others equally attractive: they all now lie sleeping in the cold ground.

The venerable Gewandhaus Hall has seen much beauty bloom and wither!

Particular cities pride themselves on the past, just as men pride themselves on their

fathers and forefathers; Leipzig did so, especially on its musical fame. No nobly-born
youth can view his pedigree with greater delight, or enumerate his succession of ancestors
with more precision, than does the *Lindenstadt* the series of great and learned Cantors
who preceded Father Sebastian at the Thomas
School, and followed him as stars do the sun.
Every exact detail was known with regard to
those " venerable gentlemen ; " and the names
of Kühnau, Schicht, and Hiller were not less
reverenced than that of Bach himself. A fair
quartette—the sisters Podleska, from Bohemia
—grateful pupils of Hiller's, erected a monument to him on the Promenade at Leipzig, a
spot which no doubt Corona Schröter often
traversed, and the student Göthe frequently
passed with Käthchen Schönkopf and Friede-
rike Oeser. It was Mendelssohn who first
originated the idea of erecting a monument to
the memory of the venerable Father of German church music, to be placed opposite the
scene of his labors, within the precincts of the
Thomas School. He forthwith applied him-

self with the greatest energy to the execution
of this scheme, and arranged a series of organ
concerts, the profits of which were to be devoted to the erection of a Bach monument.
A reverent assemblage crowded every place
and corner of the ancient, time-honored church
of St. Thomas on the 6th of August, 1840, for
the purpose of hearing Mendelssohn for the
first time play the organ. The programme
was exclusively made up of his own performances, thus devoting his powers to the fulfillment of his cherished wish. Bach's splendid
Fugue in E-flat major came first; then his
Fantasia on the Chorale "Schmücke dich, O
liebe Seele;" a Prelude and Fugue in A
minor, with twenty-one variations; the Pasto-
rella and the Trinata, in A minor; and finally,
Mendelssohn wound up the concert by extemporizing on the most deeply touching choral
melody in the world—

O Haupt voll Blut und Wunden!

No musician of the modern time was seated
above in the organ-loft. No! it was the old
and marvelous Sebastian Bach himself playing

there! Sacred awe pervaded the souls of the hearers, and tears rushed to eyes that had long since ceased to weep. The worthy old Rochlitz, who had heard Cantor Schicht play on this very organ, embraced the young master at the close of the concert, saying, "I can now depart in peace, for never shall I hear anything finer or more sublime." In my opinion, neither Mendelssohn's pianoforte nor organ-playing have been sufficiently highly estimated by his contemporaries, or possibly the *composer* in some degree drove the *practical musician* into the back-ground. Independent of the magic of his touch, which could only be *felt*, and not defined, like the charms of a night in spring, when

> Marvels that we deemed of Eld,
> Fresh in the moonshine night beheld,

and his finished technical powers, it was his *absolute* and *unqualified devotion* to the master whose work he was executing, that imparted to his playing a character of perfection that probably never was heard before, and never will be heard again. In rendering the creations of others, he introduced nothing of himself; he was entirely absorbed in the soul and spirit of the composer. At such moments he was in fact only the receptacle of precious foreign wine, but of the purest and most transparent crystal; you saw the costly liquid sparkle, and

> Swarms of spirits in upper air!
>   Sprites descend—a seething mass!
> Drinking wine, and drowning care,
>   And chinking goblets as they pass.

When I recall the impression Mendelssohn's playing made on my own young heart, I can only say that other virtuosos have often enchanted and enraptured me, such as Liszt, Klara Schumann, Ferdinand Hiller, etc; but not one of these ever inspired me with the feeling which came over me when listening to Mendelssohn. I always then felt as if I must seek out the most profound solitude, that I might continue to hear the echoes of those tones that had scarcely died away in my ear. The sweetest human voice seemed to me rough and harsh. I should have liked to be deaf for the time, so that I might hear nothing directly afterward; and my brother Edward had precisely the same feeling. At a concert where Mendelssohn played, my brother, between jest and earnest, held his hands on his ears and said, in a few minutes, " I have heard more than you, for he has played it all over again for me!" Who can tell how often these never-to-be-forgotten sounds may have recurred to the soul of the solitary pilgrim in the desert, many long years afterward, to console and to refresh him in the awful silence of that wilderness in which he was destined to find an early grave!

Even now, in some compositions that I had the good fortune to hear played by Mendelssohn, my spirit seems, when others are playing them to me, to hear distinctly *him* and *him alone*, for no other hand can efface the impression I received from his execution of particular melodies, and more especially some of his "songs without words; so at length my physical ear seems to hear those very tones once more. The senses too have their memories. The year of the Bach monument (1840) also brought to light some of Mendelssohn's grander compositions—the "Guttenberg Lied," his "Hymn of Praise," and its first performance in Leipzig. The words of the latter, consisting of texts from the Bible, put together with exquisite taste, celebrate the triumph of heavenly light over darkness. The musical composition is divided into two closely-connected portions, the great instrumental and the vocal. Who could ever forget the splendid duett for female voices, "I waited for the Lord!" with its touching close, "It is well for those who place their trust in the Lord!" A breath of gentle piety pervades the whole work, like incense in the House of God; and to that anxious question, which must find an echo in every human heart—

Watchman! will the night soon pass?

who has not sent up a kindred aspiration to heaven in the dark night of anguish and grief—

Watchman! will the night soon pass?

Like . flashing sunbeams is the answer given by a fine female voice—

The night is departing, departing

5

The double chorus that repeats the heavenly message—

The night is departing, the day is approaching !

is quite unequaled in its grandeur and devout rejoicing.

Shortly after its performance in Leipzig, Mendelssohn directed his new work in Birmingham. On his return, Leipzig heard for the first time the 42nd Psalm sung by Frau Livia Frege, who sang Mendelssohn's music with so much soul. During many months, Mendelssohn instructed a choir of zealous singers with infinite trouble, devotion, and patience, in that gigantic work, Bach's *Passionsmusik*, the performance of which took place for the benefit of the Bach monument, on the evening of Palm Sunday, 1841, in the Thomas Church. Then floated downward those deeply affecting choruses, those sacred chorals that had resounded in the same spot more than a hundred years ago; and there stood the slender figure of the young director, whose hand and eye controlled those masses of sound, where, on Good Friday, *anno* 1728, the imposing form of Sebastian Bach had stood; and the same devout emotions which then filled the souls of those hearers, whose bodies have long since moldered away into dust, now also pervaded this assembly, whose hands were folded in amazement and admiration at this giant-like composition of piety and faith. A " believing heart " alone, taken in the highest signification of the word, could thus direct and bring such a work before an audience. If the former Cantor of the Thomas School, from amid the heavenly hosts, was permitted on that Palm Sunday to listen to this earthly performance, his fiery eyes would have beamed, his heart would have exulted, over this his disciple and friend, who, after the lapse of more than a century, was more closely akin to him than even those who had sat beside him in the Cantor's dark little study, and gathered the living word from his lips.

CHAPTER VI.

BERLIN.

Wingéd warblers from each tree,
Discoursing their glad melody.

A bird in a cage wrote from Berlin, on August 9th, 1841 :—

"You wish to hear some news about the Berlin Conservatorium—so do I—but there is none. The affair is on the most extensive scale, if it be actually on any scale at all, and not merely in the air. The King seems to have a plan for reorganizing the Academy of Arts, but it is scarcely possible to effect this without entirely changing its present form into a new one, which they cannot make up their mind to do; and I am the less likely to advise this, because I do not expect much profit for music either from a formed or unformed Academy."

By desire of Friedrich Wilhelm IV., Mendelssohn left Leipzig in July, 1841, to settle in Berlin, and the above words form the beginning of a letter to his dear friend David. The art-loving King summoned the greatest of living musicians to his "Court of the Muses" as the representative of the noble science of music. In the collection of Mendelssohn's letters, we find some interesting documents on the subject of the appointment of a music director with a salary of 3,000 dollars, in an Art Academy to be instituted in Berlin, and to consist of four classes: architecture, sculpture, painting, and music. A grand music Conservatorium was to be erected, and a series of sacred and secular concerts given.

"That I am now to recommence a private life, but at the same time to become a sort of schoolmaster to a Conservatorium, is what I can scarcely realize, after my excellent, vigorous orchestra here. I might perhaps do so if I were really to enjoy an entirely private life, in which case I should only compose and live in retirement; but the mongrel Berlin doings interfere; the vast projects, the petty performances, the perfect criticism, the indifferent musicians, the liberal ideas, the Court servants in the streets, the Museum and the Academy, and the sand! I doubt whether my stay there will be more than a year; still I shall of course do all in my power not to allow this time to pass without some profit to myself and others!"

To the great joy of his mother and brother and sisters, Mendelssohn once more took possession with them of the same beloved house which (as he writes) "I quitted with a heavy heart twelve years ago." He never, however, felt at home in his native city, in spite of the efforts on all sides to make his stay in Berlin agreeable, and in every way to do honor and homage to the celebrated master. Certain individuals were indeed dear to his heart in the Berlin circles of that day, and above all, old Tieck, with his piercing eyes; Pauline von Schätzel-Decker, with her lovely voice, who sang Mendelssohn's songs with such good-will and wondrous beauty; Meyerbeer, Humboldt, Bunsen, Geibel, who was there for some weeks, Professor Wichmann, Bettina and her pretty daughters, etc. He was also much gratified by the high favor of the King, who invariably expressed himself in the most cordial manner, and always remained consistent. On the whole, however, he found the atmosphere of the "Metropolis of intelligence" oppressive. In his letters he complains that, notwithstanding his delight in living with his own family, and all his privileges and happy memories, there was no place where he felt so little at home as in Berlin. He writes to President Verkenius:

"The ground of this may be, that all the causes which formerly made it impossible for me to begin and to continue my career in Berlin, and which drove me away, still subsist, just as they formerly did, and are likely, alas! to subsist to the end of time. There is the same frittering away of all energies and all people, the same unpoetical striving after outward results, the same superfluity of perceptions, the same failure in production, and the same want of nature, the same illiberality and backwardness as to progress and development, by which, indeed, though the latter are rendered safer and less dangerous, still they are

robbed of all merit and of all life. I believe
that these qualities will one day be found again
here in all things; that it is the case with
music, there can be no doubt whatever. The
King has the best inclination to alter and to
improve all this; but even were he to hold fast
his will steadily for a succession of years, and
to find none but people with the same will,
working unweariedly in accordance with it—
even then, results and happy consequences
could not be anticipated, till *after* a succession
of years had elapsed; yet here these are expected first and foremost. The soil must be
entirely plowed and turned up before it can
bring forth fruit—so it seems to me at least in
my department. The musicians work, each for
himself, and no two agree; the amateurs are
divided and absorbed into thousands of small
circles; besides, all the music one hears is, at
the best, only indifferent; criticism alone is
keen, close, and well studied. These are no
very flattering prospects, I think, for the approaching period, and to 'organize this from
the foundation' is not my affair, for I am defi-

cient both in talent and inclination for the purpose. I am, therefore, waiting to know what is desired of me, and probably this will be limited to a certain number of concerts, which the Academy of Arts is to give in the coming winter, and which I am then to direct."

And this proved to be the case. The intellectual ruler and warm-hearted patron and protector of all the arts could not find on this occasion any whose will was in unison with his own, or who would apply their energies to carry it through; and thus all his admirable plans gradually died away, and every prospect for real practical work for Mendelssohn seemed from week to week to vanish more and more.

To escape from the burden of this conviction, he first made some excursions to Leipzig, where he both heard and shared in much good music. After Leipzig, we see him in London, living very gayly, and almost overwhelmed with honors and pleasures; "reading ' Wilhelm Meister,' " and "strolling through the fields with Klingemann to restore myself, because they really make such a fuss with me." He plays in Exeter Hall before 3,000 people, who are in transports of delight, drinks tea with Queen Victoria in the splendid gallery of Buckingham Palace, directs his "Hebrides" at the Philharmonic, hears Fanny Kemble read Shakspeare, converses with Lady Morgan and Mrs. Jameson, wanders through the galleries with Winterhalter, a celebrated painter of lace, velvet, and beautiful women ; makes music with his beloved Moscheles, with Bennett, with Duprez at Chorley's, and Benedict, and at length resolves for the next few weeks to " have nothing to do with music."

He then set off for Switzerland, where, *en route*, he was joined by Cécile, his brother, and his sister-in-law. He rested for a time in his much-loved Interlaken, proceeded to Zurich, and returned by Frankfort to his gilt cage in Berlin. It was on this journey that he wrote to his friend Hildebrandt a playful request that " his amiable wife would preserve a quantity of those capital vinegar plums, for the eating of which will gladly be answerable a certain Felix Mendelssohn."

Meanwhile, affairs in Berlin had undergone no change; and as Mendelssohn shrank from the thoughts of living on in this way, and accepting what appeared to be a sinecure, he speedily made up his mind, and requested his dismissal. It was now proposed to him that he should become the head of the Evangelical Church Music, and at the same time informed that the design was to train a select vocal choir, and a first-rate orchestra, for the artistic support of the church services, and more especially for the performance of oratorios; and this Institution was to be intrusted to his sole direction. Mendelssohn professed his readiness to undertake the work, but reserved the right of choosing his place of residence, and having the uncontrolled disposal of his time, till the realization of this noble idea was carried into effect, expressing his wish to the minister Eichhorn, to be permitted to prefer these requests in person to His Majesty. The King granted an audience to the composer of "St. Paul," expressing himself in the most gracious manner, while Mendelssohn promised his august benefactor to complete a series of compositions hereafter to be named, in accordance with the ideas of the royal personage who gave the commission, and further engaged to be on the spot as soon as "the gigantic instrument" on which he was appointed to play should be completed.

The more important works that Mendelssohn composed at the instigation of Friedrich Wilhelm IV. are the music for "The Midsummer Night's Dream," exclusive of the overture; the music for "Athalia," "Antigone," and "Œdipus von Kolonos;" and likewise a series of liturgical hymns.

With regard to his creative labors, Julius Rietz' appendix to "Mendelssohn's Letters in 1840–42," names the following:

1840.

"Hymn of Praise," Symphony Cantata, op. 52.   Leipzig.

> Performed for the first time on the 25th of June, 1840, in the Thomas Church at Leipzig, at the celebration of the Fourth Centenary of Printing.

"Festgesang," for Male Voices and Brass Band, " Begeht mit heil'gem Lobgesang."   No *opus* number.

> For the opening of the Festival in honor of Printing.

Songs for Four Male Voices:—

"Der Jäger Abschied," op. 50, no. 2.

"Wanderlied," op. 50, no. 6.

Song for Soprano, Alto, Tenor, and Bass, "Der wandernde Musikant," op. 88, no. 6.

1841.

Music for "Antigone," op. 55. Berlin.

> Performed for the first time on the 6th of November, 1841, in the New Palace, at Potsdam, and in the theater at Berlin on the 13th of April, 1842.

Variations sérieuses, for the Pianoforte, in D minor, op. 54. Leipzig.

Variations for the Pianoforte, in E-flat, op. 82. Leipzig.

Allegro brilliant for the Pianoforte, in A, arranged as a Duett, op. 92. Leipzig.

Prelude for the Pianoforte, in E minor, for "Notre Temps." Leipzig.

Songs for Voice, with Pianoforte accompaniment:—

"Frische Fahrt," op. 57, no. 6. Leipzig.

"Erster Verlust," op. 99, no. 1. Berlin.

"Das Schifflein," op. 99, no. 4. Leipzig.

Song for voice, with Pianoforte, "Ich hör' ein Vöglein locken." No *opus* number.

> Appeared first as a contribution to a Collection of Poetry by Adolph Böttger.

"Songs without Words:"—

"Volkslied," in A minor, op. 53, no. 5.

" " in A major, op. 53, no 6. } Leipzig.

" in B-flat, op. 85, no. 6

1842.

Symphony, in A minor, op. 56.   Berlin.

Called the "Scotch Symphony" in the Letters of 1830.

Songs for Voice with Pianoforte:—

 "Gondellied," op. 57, no. 5.

 "Schifflied," op. 71, no. 4.

Song for Two Voices, with Pianoforte, "Wie war so schön," op. 63, no. 2.

"Song without Words," in A major, op. 62, no. 6.

CHAPTER VII.

See ! higher in his upward march
Climbs the victorious sun.

MENDELSSOHN returned to Leipzig with the title of a Prussian General Music-Director, and in the diploma was the following annotation: "to be at the disposition of the Prussian Ministry." How often did the General Music-Director jest on the subject of this formula, and to how much amusement did it give rise in the circles of his musical friends!

The "Antigone" music was given for the first time on November 6, 1841, at the New Palace at Potsdam, and in Berlin on April 12, 1842, but did not appear in Leipzig till March 5, 1842. Frau Dessoir, an admirable actress, and Herr Reger, an able actor, exerted all their energies worthily to represent this powerful tragedy; and amid the most breathless excitement, accompanied by strains of music, the gigantic story of Destiny was seen on those boards, typical of the world " which elevates man, while showing his nothingness." This wonderful piece was three times repeated, for every one wished to see the brave heroine descend into the bridal chamber of death to rejoin the corpse of her lover.

Mendelssohn's appointment as Kapellmeister to the King of Saxony is also of this date.

A stirring migratory life now began for Mendelssohn.   He went back and forwards between Berlin, Leipzig, and Dresden, with one interlude to his beloved Düsseldorf, to attend a musical festival where Händel's " Israel in Egypt " and the " Hymn of Praise " were given; and on the third day of the festival he excited the utmost enthusiasm by his performance of Beethoven's E-flat major Concerto.

The following notice of Mendelssohn was in a musical paper, calling him " an inborn festival director:" "He combines conflicting masses, animates them to become an organized whole; and by his winning courtesy, his brilliant wit, as well as by the conspicuous treasures of his knowledge, he inspires even the most lukewarm with eager zeal, and incites the most perverse to perseverance and attention."

Honors and triumphs accompanied all his steps, and royal favor decorated his breast with the "Order of Merit." Henceforth little chance of rest was given him—all the world were laying claim to him. In spite of this outward life of excitement, he worked with his usual industry, and one bright blossom after another sprung up from his creative spirit; and yet the man so courted by all, felt himself happiest in his "little study."

How charming he writes to Klingemann at the commencement of the year 1843:—

"I now feel, however, more vividly than ever what a heavenly calling Art is; and for this also I have to thank my parents. Just when all else which ought to interest the mind appears so repugnant, and empty, and insipid, the smallest real service to Art lays hold of your inmost thoughts, leading you so far away from town, and country, and from earth itself, that it is indeed a blessing sent by God."

The Leipzig Conservatorium, for the erec-

5*

tion of which the noble King of Saxony had granted an important sum, occupied Mendelssohn very much ; and his heartfelt joy at the opening of this Institution, so fruitful in blessings for Art, is related to this day with emotion by those of his friends who were eye-witnesses of it. It had not been brought into existence without manifold cares and troubles; how much passive opposition had there been to vanquish, how many obstacles to set aside ! Mendelssohn by no means always worked under a blue sky and sunshine. Many a time his soul was wounded by narrow-mindedness, shortsightedness, ignorance and obstinacy, and above all, by irritated vanity, the outbursts of which obstructed his path in most varied forms.

The first teachers in the Leipzig Conservatorium diffused the brilliancy of their rays through all distant lands, and at a later date the venerated Moscheles was added to the number. At the commencement those who were occupied with it were Mendelssohn himself; the most learned contrapuntist in Germany, the pupil and friend of Spohr, the Cantor of the Thomas School, Moritz Hauptmann; the ever-memorable Robert Schumann; the king of violin players, David; August Pohlenz; and the celebrated organist, Becker. After the death of Pohlenz, Frau Bühnau-Grabau and Friedrich Böhme undertook the instruction in solo and choir singing. The other appointments were that amiable colleague of David, August Klengel, and two young pianoforte virtuosos, Plaidy and Wenzel. An Italian, Signor Ghezzi, agreed to teach Italian; and the clever author of "The History of Music," Franz Brendel, delivered scientific lectures to the pupils. Advocate Schleinitz, one of Mendelssohn's most devoted friends, conducted the affairs of the Institution, which soon made astonishing progress—indeed it could not be otherwise under such auspices; and it still flourishes to the glory of its founder, a genuine and legitimate seminary for the science of music.

Of the teachers at that time appointed by Mendelssohn, the following still work on in undiminished vigor:—Moscheles, David, Klengel,

Plaidy, Wenzel, and Brendel, by whose side
stand many younger talents worthy of note.

What Mendelssohn accomplished as a teacher, alone would have sufficed to gain a great
name for him; in that capacity, the grand
nature of his talents and his character appeared
in the most brilliant light. It was impossible
to show more goodness of heart and patience
than he invariably did in his intercourse with
his pupils, and his indulgence toward honest
industry and good will was most touching. On
the other hand, he was very severe toward
negligence and presumption; and to want of
truth, in whatever shape it presented itself, he
was inexorable—nay, almost implacable. He
was enthusiastically prized and idolized, but
also dreaded as the most · incorruptible of
judges. The lofty purity of his nature instinct-
ively repelled all that was ignoble—a nature
to which Göthe's words about Schiller are so
wonderfully applicable:

> And far behind him, distanced in the race,
> There lagged the vulgar curse of commonplace.

This caused him sometimes to appear blunt,

and even austere ; no one was less easily captivated by superficial brilliant qualities and
gifts, if the *inner* man did not correspond with
the glittering exterior. All his pupils acknowledged, with the warmest gratitude, how
instructive were his hints in looking through
their compositions, how suggestive his blame,
how elevating his praise. He knew how to
encourage the most apprehensive. The most
timid talent developed itself under the light
of his eyes, and blossomed like violets in sunshine ; and the most closed-up bud unfolded,
and became in *his* vicinity a glorious flower.

On the 2d of February, 1843, was performed
in the Gewandhaus Concert, and indeed for
the first time in public, Göthe's " Walpurgis
Nacht." Mendelssohn had already, in Rome,
partly composed music for this ballad, perhaps
at the express desire of Göthe ; and Hildebrandt
can still tell of many a conversation, grave and
gay, about the ancient Druids, and he no doubt
first heard that wild fantastic chorus—

Kommt mit Zacken und Gabeln,

played on the pianoforte.

The work is a musical picture in the most glowing colors—I might almost say the tints are taken from that favored land, " wo die Citronen blühen," and we breathe a spring on the *other* side of the Alps in that enchanting female chorus—

> The forest wakes to life beneath the smiles of May.

We poor creatures do not usually sing of *our* spring in such delightfully gay and buoyant strains, for generally it brings us only violent colds! Indeed, at most, our poets only dream in their poet-dens of

> That miracle of months—sweet May,
> When buds are bursting on the spray!

Alas! in the rude reality of the North these poor buds chiefly perish from *cold* — poor things!

I wonder what venerable Father Göthe would have said, could he have heard that grand and simple passage—

> ' Twixt light and darkness let us choose;
> Through foulest smoke the flame shines bright;
> What matters it if forms we lose ?
> We cannot lose thy glorious light.

As for us commonplace children of the earth,

tears rushed to our eyes, and our hearts beat with emotion. It was said in Leipzig, that on that occasion, Herr Kindermann, now in Munich, sang with inimitable beauty, and that the voice of Fräulein Schloss, in the mournful appeal of the "Frau aus dem Volke," had the most touching effect.

The years 1843 and 1844 can boast of a long list of finished compositions. We have the music of the "Midsummer Night's Dream," in which Felix Mendelssohn so clearly shows that the sportive tiny race of elves, fairies, water-sprites, and spirits of all kinds are as entirely subject to his magic scepter as to that of Oberon or his Titania. We have also the choruses and overtures to Racine's "Athalia;" a grand concert Aria for soprano; the 91st Psalm for chorus and orchestra; the 2nd, 43d, and 22nd Psalms for a choir of eight voices; a hymn for contralto, chorus, and orchestra; an anthem, "Herr Gott, du bist unsere Zuflucht," for a chorus of eight voices; several great composi-tions for pianoforte and stringed instruments; five Sonatas for the organ, books of songs,

Quartetts, Duetts; a violin Concerto in E minor, written for his dear friend and colleague David; and that most exquisite hymn for soprano, chorus, and organ, "Hör' mein Bitten, Herr, neige dich zu mir."

Mendelssohn passed the summer of 1844 in charming Soden, near Frankfort, and that city of his most delightful reminiscences detained him also all the winter. He there first thoroughly recruited his strength after all the fatigue of concerts, and the suspense of waiting and watching within the walls of Berlin. He gave himself up to the *dolce far niente* of rural life in that most attractive of all the Taunus baths, with all the gayety of a child enjoying his holidays; and how charmingly bright his mood was, we learn from a captivating letter to his sister Fanny, in which he draws a contrast between English society and his musical days in London and his present secluded life:

"If you refuse to come to Soden for a fortnight, to enjoy with me the incredible fascinations of this country and locality, all my descriptions are of no avail; and, alas! I know too well that you will not come. I therefore spare you many descriptions. My family improve every day in health, while I lie under apple-trees and huge oaks. In the latter case, I request the swine-herd to drive his animals under some other tree, not to disturb me (this happened yesterday); further, I eat strawberries with my coffee, at dinner and supper; I drink Asmannshäuser, rise at six o'clock, and yet sleep nine hours and a half (pray, Fanny, at what hour do I go to bed?) I visit all the wondrously beautiful environs, and meet Herr B—— in the most romantic spot of all (happened yesterday), who gives me the latest and best report of you all, and addresses me as General Music-Director, which sounds to me as strange here as Oberursel, and Lorschbach, and Schneidhein would to you. Then toward evening I have visits from Lenau, and Hoffmann von Fallersleben, at Freiligrath, when we stroll through the fields for a quarter of an hour, near home, and find fault with the system of the world, utter prophecies about the weather, and are unable to say what is to become of England in the future. Further, I sketch busily, and compose still more busily."

And in another letter to Fanny Hensel, a longing sigh seems breathed from the very depth of his heart:

"If I could only continue to live during half a year as I have done here for a fortnight past, what might I not accomplish? But the regulation and direction of so many concerts, and attending others, give me no pleasure, and produce no result."

Indeed, he did not even here succeed in living as unnoticed as he wished; those he knew and did not know, equally sought him out, and musical celebrities made pilgrimages to Soden in order to see him; vocal societies brought their *vivat*, and meanwhile Mendelssohn directed a musical festival in the Palatinate, where he was much made of, and where his "St. Paul" and "Walpurgis Nacht" were performed. Letters innumerable from all parts told him of that busy world without, that he would so gladly have forgotten. When, however, he had heard and read enough, he used suddenly to disappear, and lie down again under his favorite apple-trees, his music and drawing portfolios beside him, gazing into the green twilight of the forest, watching the rays of light darting across the turf, and listening to a medley of birds, singing in every key, and yet always in perfect harmony, never out of tune and never out of time. And gradually all became darker and stiller. The moon rose, while strange distant chimes and the low tremulous tones of horns stole on the ear. The air was full of ringing and stirring life; wings gently rustled in flying past, and elves darted rapidly past on their tiny white steeds with golden antlers, while their lovely queen nodded to him "smiling as she rode by."

But not only does Mendelssohn appear to have passed a happy summer in Frankfort, but also a joyous winter. How full of fun is that passage in a letter to Rebecca Dirichlet, dispatched from Frankfort, the City on the Maine, to Florence, the City on the Arno—Fanny Hensel being then in Rome:

"I came with S—— last night at one

o'clock from a musical punch party, where I first played Beethoven's Sonata 106, in B-flat, and then drank 212 glasses of punch *fortissimo*. We sang the duett from ' Faust ' in the Mainz Street, because there was such wonderful moonlight, and to-day I have rather a headache. Pray, cut off this part before you send this letter to Rome; a younger sister may be intrusted with such a confidence; but an elder one, and in such a Papal atmosphere— not for your life ! "

Mendelssohn seems at that period to have thought seriously of subsequently settling in Frankfort. In a letter to the worthy Senator Bernus, written from Leipzig, October 10, 1845, he says :—

" As soon, however, as I have won the right to live solely for my inward work and composing, only occasionally conducting and playing in public just as it may suit me, then I shall assuredly return to the Rhine, and probably, according to my present idea, settle at Frankfort. The sooner I can do so, the more I shall be pleased. I never undertook external musical pursuits, such as conducting, etc., from inclination, but only from a sense of duty; so I hope, before many years are over, to apply myself to building a house."

A host of birds of passage from distant lands, and passing scholars, flocked to the master at Leipzig during the winter of 1845–46. The most far-famed representatives of music were to be seen and heard in the *Lindenstadt*. Hector Berlioz, Keller, Pauline Garcia, M'me Schröder and her daughter, and the talented Wilhelmine Devrient; Gade, a young Dane, the clever composer of that Highland Symphony with which Mendelssohn was so highly delighted; the admired pianist, M'me Dulcken (David's sister); Parish Alvars, Servais, Robert Franz from Halle, Lobe from Vienna, and many others. Among the casual pupils I include Louis Ehlert from Königsberg, the author of "Musical Letters and Diaries from Rome;" Richard Wuerst, Karl Reinecke, Riccius, Otto Goldschmidt; that inseparable couple of violinists, Joseph von Wasielewsky and Otto von Königslöw, the former of whom has taken a place among authors as the biographer of Schumann, the latter being a concert meister; Otto Dresel, now in America as a propagandist of German music; and likewise a certain virtuoso, then very juvenile, in a short Hungarian jacket—Joseph Joachim by name!

Amid all these musicians some poets start forth, who in those days, as they moved along, seemed in my eyes encompassed with golden halos, such as we see round the heads of saints. Which of these could ever have imagined that the merry young girl to whom they said a few good-humored words in passing, or sometimes asked to sing for them, or danced with her, as, for example, the author of the " Village Tales of the Black Forest," would one day have the privilege to address them as her " colleague? "

Gustav Freytag lived in Leipzig, the elegant Robert Heller, and also Heinrich Laube, Oswald Marbach, Julius Hammer, Hermann Marggraff, Gustav Kühne, Moritz Hartmann, whose handsome poetical head we all secretly so much admired; Andersen also often came over; and also the *enfant chéri* of the Leipzig ladies, the renowned Berthold Auerbach. An ardent enthusiast for music, a most delightful member of society, he belonged specially to that circle of which Mendelssohn formed the brilliant center. Legationsrath Gerhard, the masterly translator of Burns, moved amid all these his colleagues with youthful freshness and sensibility.

In many Leipzig families the musical element reigned in the most cheerful sociability, above all in the house of Karl Harkort, at whose hospitable gatherings mighty minds did indeed sometimes come into collision, as friend and foe alike met there. Frau Auguste Harkort, Gustav Kühne's mother-in-law, the most intellectual and warm-hearted of women, and formerly a distinguished singer, did the honors of the most charming *salon*, where there were readings, music, theatricals, dinners, and suppers; she gave fêtes to young and old in Leipzig; and also in her pretty little country-house at Dölitz, receiving all her guests with the utmost courtesy. May her quiet grave in the beautiful churchyard of the Johann Church never be without an ivy-wreath, in grateful remembrance of so many happy hours!

The excellent Prince Reuss habitually received the representatives of art, poetry, and science, and so did the brothers Härtel, the respected proprietors of the world-famed firm of Breitkopf & Härtel; there was also the worthy couple Dörrien, Hofrath Keil, the houses of Preusser, Salomon-Seeburg, Kistner, Consul Clauss, Petschke, Friedrich and Heinrich Brockhaus, Von der Pfordten, the *Rector magnificus* of that day. The most refined of all musical enjoyments, however, under the aegis of the sweet vocal muse, was offered in the salon of Frau Livia Frege; a choice selection of music in every style was to be heard in Reudnitz, at the house of the interesting old Friedrich Hofmeister, the hospitable, amiable patron of all rising musical talent.

On a certain day late in the autumn of 1845, in the first floor of the Bürger School, one forenoon, at twelve o'clock, Kapellmeister Mendelssohn was announced. We certainly were in some degree prepared for this visit, for Ferdinand Böhme, my singing - master, whom I remember with gratitude, told me he had spoken to Mendelssohn of my zeal for music, and of my voice, and that his reply was, "I will go myself shortly, and have a look at this little singing-bird." If the mere suggestion excited me so much, and even caused me sleepless nights, the announcement of the actual presence of him I had expected brought on a paroxysm of fever! My sisters gathered round me; we could scarcely realize that there, in the adjoining room, was actually the man whose praises we sang in every key. My parents, too, were not quite composed; my mother's sweet, fragile face changed color, but she summoned sufficient courage to open the door between us and our valued guest—and that I believe I could not have brought myself to do in the course of an hour. I followed them into the room is if in a dream, while my sisters, as I well knew, peeped through the keyhole by turns.

He came up to us in as friendly a manner as if we had been old acquaintances, and shook

hands with my father; we sat down beside
him, when he began to chat with my parents,
telling them he had heard much praise of my
voice and my soul for music, from my teacher;
that he, as well as the public, at this moment
stood in need of fresh voices and musical talent, and that all, according to the powers allot-
ted to them, must contribute to further the
cause of music—that the Concert Hall of the
Gewandhaus was no battle-field, but an artistic
Institution, where youthful rising genius was
offered an opportunity to learn something solid.
One word gave rise to another; my father and
mother also spoke; and although the latter, to
all the persuasions of my singing-master to
allow me to study art as a profession, had en-
ergetically answered, "Never can I consent
that my child should appear in public!" I
now saw and heard, to my amazement, that,
fairly vanquished, she placed this same child
at the disposition of the Herr Kapellmeister.
The opposition of my father also was only
feeble, and speedily overcome. Mendelssohn,
indeed, always carried his point; no one could

ever withstand his manner, his glance, or his smile; as for myself, I was of course ready to do everything—to sing day and night if he thought it advisable. We would all have gone through real fire and water for him—not, like Tamino and Pamina, through merely painted flames; but on no account would I have allowed this to be remarked. On this occasion, therefore, I sat quite still and silent, gazing at the charming refined countenance, and listening, as if in a dream, to his gentle voice and rapid, eager utterance.

He then suddenly turned to the "little singing-bird," and said, with a smile, "Will you be so good as to sing something for me! I should like so much to hear you."

I felt my heart stop beating, and I became as pale as death; but I stood up and replied, "If you wish it, I will try."

"What music is that on the piano?"—and at these words he rose. "May I look at it? I hope you are not frightened?"

I looked at him and encountered such a kindly smile, that I suddenly regained my courage. It also occurred to me how soundly my good master would scold me if I did not do him credit, and in all my life I never could endure being scolded. "Here are Mozart's 'Zauberflöte,' and Mendelssohn's 'St. Paul,'" said I.

"And here is the 'Creation,' portions of which we are soon to perform," rejoined Mendelssohn; "I think we are in very interesting society. Pray sing me the Aria 'Jerusalem.'"

Alas! just as if he really had been aware of it—the very Aria in which Herr Böhme always found fault with me, on account of a mistake I often made in the time, and which required such calmness and long breath. But my mood was like that of Möros, when he says to Dionysius:—

I am prepared for death,
Not for the alms of life;

so, without any remonstrance, I placed the Aria on the music-desk.

Mendelssohn seated himself at the piano, and after preluding for a few minutes, he nodded to me as a signal to begin.

I remember that I neither knew *who* I was, nor *where* I was. I only thought, "It is Mendelssohn who is accompanying you, and you are to sing something out of ' St. Paul.' "

And I sang. On this occasion I made no mistake in the time; but the F, which I ought to have held steadily, trembled sadly at the commencement; but the longer I went on, the more calm and composed I felt; and only toward the close, when I again thought of what was yet to come—*his* verdict—did my voice once more tremble. But all my alarm proved superfluous; he was most kind and encouraging, commending the freshness of my voice and warmth of expression. " I hope you will very often sing for us," said he; " you must frequent the society of Fräulein Schloss, and then we shall hear some beautiful duetts!" At the same time he requested me to study the Aria out of the " Creation," " With verdure clad thy fields appear," and also to undertake an Elfin part in the approaching performance of the " Midsummer Night's Dream," for my first *début* in the Gewandhaus. Behold me then one evening, in suitable Elfin attire, all in white, beside my sister Elf, Fräulien Schwarzbach (subsequently a singer in Munich), on the raised platform of the momentous Concert Hall. The sweet intoxicating music of the "Midsummer Night's Dream" floated and undulated round me, and then I sang my "Spotted Snakes" and my bright "Good Night!" My eyes were steadily fixed on the director; and though my heart beat violently, my voice did not tremble; and my father, who had taken refuge in the furthest corner of the large center box occupied by those stern judges, the members of the Concert Direction, came afterward, with a cheerful smile, to fetch his "Elf." From my first moment to the present hour, counting and reckoning have ever been a *point noir* to me; so my admirable teacher, who no doubt believed that I should be sure to go wrong in the time, now looked quite radiant.

He, however, was *satisfied*, and said, with his sunny smile, that my *début* was a brilliant one. The very next morning—for which I shall ever be grateful to him—Mendelssohn

came to see my mother, who, in her anxiety
and tenderness, could not bear to hear me sing
before so many strangers, and never could
eventually be persuaded to do so. He spoke
with such warmth and kindness of the little
" Elf," that she was affected even to tears.
This was only another of those innumerable
instances of that "courtesy of heart," the
effects of which are so inexpressibly cheering.
Who, save Mendelssohn, would, in this charming manner, have taken any trouble about the
début of a beginner?

From that day I took a certain share in the
best public and private musical life of Leipzig,
was entitled to "have my say," and for a time
floated with the stream—

Blinded by excess of light.

I also at that time frequented the society of
Fräulein Schloss, not a little elated at being
permitted to do so. She lived at that period
in the Place de Repos, and was engaged for a
second concert season in Leipzig; and how
amiably she received her future colleague, how
cordially and charmingly she knew how to in-

spire me with courage, how admirably she
assisted me in my studies! My reminiscences
of her and her sympathetic voice, of her modesty and cheerfulness, her reverence for Mendelssohn, and of our ductts great and small,
which sounded as if cast in one mold, are
among the brightest of those golden days.
And yet all the other artistic forms who at
that time so kindly helped to encourage the
young novice in art, still rise vividly before
me:—Moscheles, in all his goodness, and his
beautiful and universally beloved and revered
wife ; David, so cheerful and intelligent, whose
critical eye we so nervously sought; Gade, the
amiable conductor, whose head recalled the
portraits of Mozart, and whose personal appearance enchanted the ladies of Leipzig, who
liked dancing so much, but who did not merely
dance (to use his own playful simile) like a
commode, but with the spirit and gayety of a
student; Hauptmann, the composer of the
" Salve Regina," and those charming songs,
with violin accompaniment, that his wife sang
with such depth of feeling; Julius Rietz, Fer-

dinand Hiller, Lobe, Ernst Richter, and Robert Franz. I had but a passing glimpse of Robert Schumann at that time; he was settled in Dresden, and only occasionally came to Leipzig when any of his works were performed—as, for instance, his "Paradise and the Peri"—or when his accomplished wife played.

A great deal of good music was given in private circles during that winter in Leipzig, and it was not confined to the families of the Mendelssohns, Moscheles, Davids, and Schleinitz. Wherever people were collected, trios, choruses from oratorios, and quartettes of all kinds were performed on the spur of the moment.

On similar occasions, and more especially in the charming Sunday *matinées* at M. Frege's, Frau Livia Frege exerted her sweet voice; there, too, the good-humored, jovial old Herr Limburger sang Zelter's ballads with inimitable liveliness and spirit; while in quartettes, the clear soprano of Fräulein Jenny Küstner, and the melodious tenor of Herr Emil Trefftz, were specially excellent; and when Mendelssohn was present, he never in all the crowd overlooked his young " recruit ; "—however closely he was surrounded, he always found a moment to address a friendly word to us, a playful question or jest as he passed.

I have heard complaints of Mendelssohn's bluntness, and want of amiability in social life. It was said that he often sat stiff and silent, without allowing a single spark to escape of the fire and genius in his nature, so well known to all his friends. But then how people harassed him, who was so averse to all ovations! How they persisted in inviting him to luxurious feasts, that his name might shed a luster on their salons, without caring to bring any sympathetic element into contact with him! How was he persecuted by applications of every kind, which he found himself constrained to refuse; and this, indeed, produced angry faces and spiteful inuendoes. He could be very irritable when people thought they were bound to converse with him exclusively about *music;* in the same way that nothing is more depressing to an author, than to make his works the incessant topic of conversation. "As if I were incapable of talking on any other subject than my profession," said he, sometimes with amusing indignation.

How animated, on the other hand, did he become in any discussion on scientific or literary subjects; how completely was he at home on every topic, owing to his rare and universal culture, and his profound and lively interest in all the higher questions connected with the realms of art and science; how delighted were the old gentlemen, celebrated professors, rectors, and directors, in the venerable Leipzig, to converse with him! On the other hand, political discussions, which in those turbulent times were scarcely to be avoided among men, were apt to annoy him; and his friend Berthold Auerbach, who in his vivacity sometimes touched on this combustible subject, was apt to come pretty sharply into collision with him.

I may here make mention of the "Liedertafel," as an attempt to bring about closer union in the different circles formed in Leipzig for the furtherance of music and sociability, although its existence was a very ephemeral one. Members of the better classes and the aristocracy assembled in a large room on the first story of the Aeckerlein House in the market-place, where no one acted the part of either host or guest. The whole company without distinction sang quartettes, and afterward supped together; but though Göthe says—

> I love my Leipzig,
> 'Tis a small Paris nurturing her sons,

still, unluckily, even to the present day it only remains a "*small* Paris," where there is much that cannot be effected by any skill or efforts, which in large Paris would have come of itself. The genuine Leipziger does not choose to be molded; his own individuality must suffice to cast a halo around him. It is well known that innumerable "kings of the rats" resided in Leipzig, to whose tails clung a faithful band; and the cost of bringing all these arbitrary despots within the folds of *one* Liedertafel, those who made the attempt to establish this grand scheme of fraternity were only too soon to discover. Each person who paid his contribution arrived with a feeling of supreme contempt for his rival in the Aeckerlein Hall, and quite determined for no consideration in the world to abate an atom of his own dignity; and as for the thoughts of the "queens of the rats," we dare not attempt to portray them. It was therefore inevitable that the large circle should be split into innumerable smaller ones; those alone who daily associated with each other still held together, and only a very few bold navigators hazarded themselves on those unknown seas.

Mendelssohn, as one independent of all coteries, did the honors in the most charming manner, cheerfully assisted by Gade and David. How many playful and memorable words they addressed to me; and sometimes Mendelssohn would whisper, " What as to the time of that pretty passage? " when he sang in a scarcely audible voice some difficult passage in an Aria which I was perhaps studying at that very moment, or beat time while I sang it over *piano-pianissimo.* We young girls, who on those occasions usually flocked together, always took the greatest trouble with the quartettes; for at all events while we were singing, all discord ceased, and then he would sometimes say, "I distinctly heard how very well those in this little corner sang!" and we all recommenced with fresh ardor after such an eulogium.

When the time for supper arrived, however, our old schisms revived:

Disperse! disperse! ye valiant men,

was our silent watchword, and small groups clung steadily to each other, gave mutual toasts, and whispered together so that their neighbors should not hear them. The new Leipzig "Liedertafel," therefore, in spite of every attempt to save it, died a natural death during the ensuing winter. No words can describe Mendelssohn's exceeding kindness to me, when I sang at the Gewandhaus. He moved his conductor's desk forward, which was quite unusual, so that it was close beside me, and I could see him just before me in order to inspire me with courage, and how good-naturedly he nodded and glanced at me while conducting! When I was sitting in the place appropriated to the singers in front of the orchestra, and my turn came to sing, my heart beat so violently, that during the previous overture I could distinguish no notes, but felt only a buzzing, rushing sound in my ears; when a pause arrived, he used to come down the steps that led from the platform to the place where the audience sat. With that easy grace which so well became him, he made a bow, and I followed him to the platform with sensations closely allied to those of the condemned criminal when he ascends the scaffold. How many hundred eyes were directed toward me! But Mendelssohn had always a cheering word for the timid singer. "Mademoiselle, you always do your work so admirably; but I can see by your face this evening that you intend fairly to bewitch the public;" or, "Now just for the next half-hour imagine that you are the first singer in Europe; and so will I;" or, "Let us try to turn Ferdinand Böhme's head altogether to-day with delight!" Oh!

who could ever forget all those kind words, and the kind face too!

I went once to see him with Sophie Schloss, to sing Reichardt's " Violet " Duett—a simple, sweet melody, "Ein Veilchen auf der Wiese stand." I had the first part, and took the high B-flat with perfect ease and courage. On which he turned to me and said, with a bright glance, " Charmingly sung indeed, and it goes straight to the heart! If Reichardt could only hear you! I must write to his daughter about it. How innocent and lovely it sounds, and how beautifully the voices blend! I could listen to it for hours!" It was on this occasion that he gave us a little duett on the words " Thou hast me forsaken, Jamie." Fräulein Schloss sang, " Thou hast me *forgotten*, Jamie." "*Forsaken*," repeated Mendelssohn, adding, " After all, it is pretty much the same thing. To be forsaken is to be forgotten; what do you say, ladies?" "Oh! I think that to be forgotten must be a thousand times worse than to be forsaken," said I. Mendelssohn turned, and, looking at me, said with fervor, "Only see the lesson that little girl gives us both; and how right she is! To be forsaken is hard to bear; but to be forgotten, the saddest thing in the world!"

The concert in which we sang this "Violet" song in public was particularly brilliant, and Mendelssohn in his most radiant mood. Sophie Schloss was in yellow satin and black lace, with dark crimson roses in her hair. She first sang with the most enthusiastic applause Mozart's "Violet," an especial favorite of Mendelssohn's; and then came our "Violet" Duett, which was three times encored; the Trio from Cimarosa's "Matrimonio Segreto," in which Fidalma (Schloss), with her soothing "Vergogna—vergogna!" excelled to the uttermost, while I almost *acted* the part of the excited Karoline, to Mendelssohn's very great satisfaction, for I sang with so much fire; and the third in our bond, Fräulein Starke, was full of vivacity; so this exquisite piece of music was also uproariously encored. On that evening, Mendelssohn said to Sophie Schloss, "We

6*

have a pretty little *Wald Schloss* here, but our little *Concert Schloss* is by far prettier."

When I took leave of him he said, "I cannot forget the 'Violet' song; and the first time that I am sad at heart, I will beg you to sing it for me."

It is most pleasing to read in Sophie Schloss' letters, written in her own delightful manner, the details of her residence at that time in Leipzig, and of her intimacy with Mendelssohn. She was attached to him with the most devoted gratitude. He was her friend and teacher, and promoted her splendid talent in every possible way. By his warm recommendations she received the most flattering and lucrative offers on all sides to sing at concerts, while he obtained permission for her from the Directors of the Leipzig Concerts to accept these engagements. Once, when she returned to Leipzig after a prolonged tour of concerts, and went to see Mendelssohn, he called out to her, laughing, "Fräulein Schloss, you are come home again, like the 'Dorf-Barbier!'" She always sang to him previous to every grand rehearsal, when he would not allow her to leave him until she could execute the music in question exactly in accordance with his ideas. Ah! these were indeed charming days! but Fräulein Schloss writes, " I had my evil days too! " On one occasion she had to sing to him at first sight, and transpose an Aria of Mozart's (the same that David afterward played so splendidly). The singer herself admits that "it went as badly as possible; " on which Mendelssohn at length started up and tore the Aria into a hundred pieces. " Horrible! beneath all criticism! " he exclaimed. Sophie Schloss' large dark eyes, that had watched his movements in alarm, now filled with tears, and the much admired singer began to weep bitterly. Then Mendelssohn came up to her, and laying his hand gently on her shoulder, asked, " Why do you weep?—was I too abrupt? Now pray be calm again. You shall have a song for your album to make up for it, and to-morrow we shall no doubt sing better."

And accordingly she received from him a lovely song, with the subscription, " From your very great and sincere—perhaps *too* sincere—admirer."

One day she appeared at the rehearsal with long curls, instead of her hair being smoothly dressed as usual. She was at once conscious, by his glance, that something in her displeased him, for he was rather ungracious. When the rehearsal was over, she frankly asked him the cause of his being out of humor. "Your curls provoke me, Fräulein Schloss," was the reply. "Wear your hair smooth; curls ought never to be black, but light, brown, or fair!"

The printed list of Mendelssohn's works of that date is as follows:

Music for Œdipus; Quintett for stringed instruments; five organ Sonatas; Songs for one voice with pianoforte, and Songs without words; Cantata to the "Sons of Art," for the Cologne Festival; a *Lauda Sion* for chorus, solo, and orchestra; Songs for four male voices; Anthems for an eight-part chorus, and the Oratorio of "Elijah." The text-book of the latter grand work of Mendelssohn is compiled from the First Book of Kings. It first brings forward Elijah's prophecy of famine, and the lamentations of the sufferers; then the journey of the Prophet; the splendid scene between him and the widow, which ends with the revival of the child; the destruction of the priests of Baal; the prayer for rain, a passage of marvelous effect; "Behold! there ariseth a little cloud out of the sea," sung by a tender boyish voice; the opening of the heavens, and the bursting forth of the waters. The second part consists of the persecution and flight of Elijah into the wilderness, his ascension to heaven, and his prediction of the Messiah. Independent of the effect produced by the noble choruses, the female vocal Trio, without accompaniment, "Lift up thine eyes!" has a truly magic charm. Gumprecht beautifully says of this last grand creation of Mendelssohn's: "'St. Paul' was the work of a youth of five-and-twenty; whereas in the "Elijah," separated by a space of ten years from the former, the complete man stands before us, of fully matured intellect, whose sole object now is, by his artistic productions, to repay to the

world, and to life, what they formerly bestowed
on him in inner and outer impressions and experience.   The voice of the Prophet is indeed
a hammer that cleaves rocks asunder.   Händel's triumphal and powerful style finds here
a mighty echo; and not less does the spirit of
that ancient master sweep past us in the proud
eagle flight of the choruses."

During the last winter of Mendelssohn's active labors in the concerts of the Gewandhaus,
the apparition of *Jenny Lind* fell like a ray
of light in the chequered world of phenomena.

> There is a high and holy band
> Whose inspiration needs no guide,
> No ancestry of power and pride,
> To lead them to the promised land,

says Voltaire.   And such a being was the
fair Swede, whose youthful history Charlotte
Birch-Pfeiffer has so poetically described.
Even when still a child of three, she seemed
the lark of her parents' dusky house; as a girl
of nine, she attracted the attention of all lovers
of music, and entered the Conservatorium of
Stockholm as a pupil, where her charming

voice, her fine ear, her marvelous musical memory, her industry, and her captivating modesty, made her the favorite of her singing-master—the most meritorious of musicians and composers—Berg. She appeared in various childish parts, written expressly for her, and the public was enchanted with the silvery tones that streamed from the lips of the little fairy. Probably her continuous studies at so tender an age was the cause of her sudden loss of voice, to the horror of her teacher. During four long years did Jenny Lind, with astonishing perseverance, pursue her theoretical and technical musical studies in spite of her organ being almost extinct; and then the full sweet sounds came back almost as suddenly as they had vanished. Her faithful master greeted with delight the melting tones of that sweet voice of which his beloved pupil had been so long deprived, and again brought her forward in triumph before the astonished public. She appeared as Agathe, in Weber's "Freischütz," amid an unparalleled storm of applause and delight. But there burned within her soul the longing to learn more, to hear more; the wings of this great artistic soul fluttered impatiently; the limits were too confined; so Jenny Lind went to Paris, in order to study with Manuel Garcia, the accomplished brother of Malibran and Pauline Viardot, those wondrous double stars in the firmament of vocal art. The severance from her home, the fatigue of the journey, and a feeling of isolation affected the tender organ of the young girl to such an extent that the celebrated maestro, after having tried the voice of his new pupil, uttered that well-known verdict, "*Mon enfant, vous n'avez plus de voix!* Take entire rest for three months, exercise your voice with caution—*et puis je serai charmé de vous revoir !*"

A quiet tearful year ensued—a year of hopeless study, of deepest sorrow, and ardent longing for home. After the lapse of three months Jenny Lind began to study, with incomparable energy, under the direction of Garcia, day by day, shedding tears on her pillow at night, and dreaming of her distant home; but, amid all her dreams, she seemed always to hear that pitiless voice, saying, "*mon enfant, vous n'avez plus de voix!*" Like the young palm-tree, however, under the pressure of the heavy rock, which every one thought must have crushed it, so did this regal talent continue to shoot upward to the blue sky, under the weight of home-sickness. Still, no word of praise escaped Garcia's lips; he only commended the industry, perseverance, and the facile organ of his pale, quiet pupil, whose voice appeared to him irremediably injured and feeble. Many other brilliant vocal talents, too, were at that very time blooming in his *parterre*, before whose glowing tints the delicate water-lily paled.

It was reserved for a grand and fervent artistic soul to discover her value, and to transport her from darkness into light. Searching artistic eyes found her out; the most exquisite artistic ear felt the ineffable magic of her voice. To Giacomo Meyerbeer the world is indebted for the gift of Jenny Lind. He heard her one evening sing Alice's Aria in

"Robert," "*Va, va, dit-elle, mon enfant!*" and was deeply moved. No other voice had ever conveyed this sweet and tender entreaty of a dying mother to her son with such touching fervor; it became almost a prayer, and the composer of "Robert" felt that it was tones such as these that had floated in his soul when he wrote down that "last greeting from a departing soul."

Jenny Lind now returned for a short space to her northern home in order previously to study the German language in Dresden, and to prepare in entire seclusion for her first appearance in Berlin.

In October, 1844, she made her *début* in the Royal Opera House as "Norma," and then as Vielka, in Meyerbeer's "Feldlager," exciting a degree of enthusiasm quite unparalleled on those boards either before or since.

When she appeared in Leipzig, on December 4, 1845, the concert public were in a state of feverish excitement; and when at length she came forward on the raised platform, a slender girlish form with luxuriant fair hair, dressed in pink silk, and white and pink camelias on her breast and in her hair, in all the chaste grace of her deportment, and so utterly devoid of all pretension, the spell was dissolved, and the most joyous acclamations ensued.

Jenny Lind only looked beautiful when she sang, and also in the portrait done of her by Magnus in Berlin, now in the possession of Professor Wichmann, and which may well be called a *glorified* one. She was pale, and had no freshness of complexion, nor were her features either regular or in any way remarkable. Music alone, and nothing else, transfigured her countenance so wonderfully; it then became actually transparent, the soul within shining brightly through the earthly vail in the most enchanting manner.

And it was thus she sang, on that evening in the Gewandhaus, Bellini's "Casta Diva," the Duett from the "Montecchi e Capuletti," "Se fuggire," with Miss Dolby, the letter Aria from Mozart's "Don Juan," and two of Mendelssohn's songs, "Auf Flügeln des Gesanges," and "Leise zieht durch mein Gemüth."

I cannot remember how I got home after that concert; I only know that I trembled and wept, and never closed my eyes all night. It was not, however, the " Casta Diva," with all its pearly adornment and florid graces, not the lovely Giulietta, nor the stately Donna Anna who haunted my thoughts, and whom I seemed ever to hear; it was exclusively the ineffably sweet, ethereal, almost unearthly, "By the first rose thou hap'st to meet." And what must Mendelssohn have felt, who was seated at the piano, accompanying the singer, and from whose soul this lovely flower of song had sprung.

Next day, Jenny Lind gave another concert, this time for the benefit of the Leipzig Orchestral Widows' Fund. She sang the grand Aria of the Countess in Mozart's "Figaro," "E Susanna non vien," the Freischütz Aria, "Wie nähte mir der Schlummer," the finale of "Euryanthe," "Sehnenverlangen," and some Swedish airs. Mendelssohn played his G minor Concerto, and the sixth "Song without Words," first book. I thought I had never heard him play more beautifully.

Inexpressibly touching was the mournful "Dove sono" of Jenny Lind; how chaste and simple, "Leise, leise, from me Weise," and how inspiriting the joyous words, "Alle meine Pulse schlagen!" And the roulades of the finale, too, were enchanting, and the high C bright as a sunbeam; and lovely beyond measure her native melodies; but nothing on that evening affected me, or probably ever will affect me so deeply as that "Leise zieht durch mein Gemüth."

At the close of this concert I chanced, in the pressure of the crowd, to be close to Mendelssohn; and as he had always a kind look for all in any way connected with him, he remarked me, and said with a smile, "So! I see you are quite pale from actual delight! You intend to learn to sing like that, too, don't you?"

At a later date, when I once said to him, that, since hearing Jenny Lind, I should like to study day and night, he eagerly rejoined, "Well done! you are right! the soul that feels *discouraged* in the presence of real greatness will never become thoroughly artistic.

We must ever strive after the_ *highest* aims, and *never* become weary, or allow our wings idly to droop, merely because others have earlier than ourselves attained the goal to which we aspire!"

It was after that concert, too, that Mendelssohn made his appearance as a public speaker, as we learn from the diary of an eye-witness, to whom we are indebted for this interesting account.

Jenny Lind, who was staying with her connections, the Brockhaus family, had received a deputation from the Directors of the Gewandhaus Concerts, in grateful acknowledgment of her services, followed by a torch-light serenade, as a tribute to the admired singer, in which so large a portion of the public were interested, that the spacious court-yard of the Brockhaus mansion was entirely filled. Weber's "Jubel Ouverture" was performed, succeeded by various songs. Quite perplexed by this ovation, Jenny Lind asked Mendelssohn what she ought to do with these people! Mendelssohn advised her to go down and thank them herself in a few words, if she wished to cause real pleasure to the musicians. " Very well," said she, after a pause, " I will go to them, but you must accompany me, and speak for me."

Mendelssohn instantly offered her his arm, and escorted her into the circle of performers, who greeted the appearance of their two favorites together, with a burst of applause. Mendelssohn then spoke as follows :—" Gentlemen ! You must not think that I am Mendelssohn, for at this moment I am Jenny Lind, and as such I thank you from my heart for your delightful surprise. Having now, however, fulfilled my honorable commission, I am again transformed into the Leipzig Music-Director, and in that capacity I say, Long live Jenny Lind ! ! "

A thousandfold echo responded to this call; the charming and ready manner in which he had just addressed them, exciting the most lively enthusiasm, however eagerly Fräulein Lind protested against such a mode of fulfilling her commission. The singers dispersed to the strains of Mendelssohn's "Waldlied." It was a memorable scene.

Jenny Lind, so different in her personality from all other artists, soon became, in her girlish modesty, and spotless purity and disinterestedness, a kind of mythical form to the public at large. Fable after fable was related about her, and at length it would scarcely have seemed marvelous had she dissolved into mist before all eyes, or floated away like her own *piano-pianissimo.* Some maintained that she had fallen a prey to everlasting sorrow, having lost the love of her youth by death. Others asserted positively that she had been betrothed to a young village pastor in Sweden, who had forsaken her when she went on the stage. Some declared, still more confidently, that she had refused the hands of various princes, and that she had made a vow, out of gratitude, to become the wife of her first teacher in Stockholm, etc. In fact, the most incredible things were resorted to, in order to explain the spell that she cast over all who heard her. Jenny Lind's true spell consisted, in my opinion, in three things: in the perfection of her technical culture—perfection to an extent that caused the most finished art to appear the most finished nature; in the soul that vibrated in her tones; and in the charm of a peculiar *voix voilée* and inimitably tender organ. Her *piano* was a *breath*, such as angelic lips might breathe. Those who listened to her felt as if there was something holy in the art of singing, and that this "Mädchen aus der Fremde" had only come among us to proclaim the truth to the children of this world. I never heard Jenny Lind after that evening; but every time I think of her, there rings in my memory—

By the first rose thou hap'st to meet,
Send fondest greetings to my sweet.

During the various visits, short and long, of Mendelssohn to Berlin, he made much music with Jenny Lind. They also met at Aix, during the Musical Festival there. It must have been a matchless intellectual enjoyment to both to listen to each other, and to feel, moreover, that they were journeying on the same path, mutually cherishing the highest ideal of Art in their hearts, and that they looked upward with the same devout earnestness of purpose—identical in their faith in the Divinity of Art.

In the hospitable house of Professor Wichmann, in Berlin, Mendelssohn was in the habit of meeting Jenny Lind, and accompanying her songs. There, too, concerts on a grander scale were often arranged, and attended by the highest *élite* of the Berlin musical world, but far more frequently confined to a small circle of choice spirits, for whom Mendelssohn extemporized, and Jenny Lind sang her favorite songs and arias. How happy were those privileged to listen! These two artistic souls were in perfect harmony—they completed each other so wonderfully; his own musical ideas, as well as those of the master whom he revered the most, found their thorough expression by her voice. It was a rare combination of two innately congenial natures.

I believe it was the appearance of Jenny Lind on the stage that once more powerfully revived Mendelssohn's ardent wish to write an

Opera in a grand style. What an attractive conception to compose a work the representative of which should be this noble woman and her magic voice!

Even while in Düsseldorf, Mendelssohn cherished in his heart a longing for an effective opera-text, and at that time alluded to a new opera composition that was to be "something fresh and gay." Subsequently, to various friends, such as Devrient, Holtei, and Spohr, both verbally and in writing, he lamented his difficulty: "I would so gladly write an Opera, but, far or near, I neither can find a text nor a poet." He indeed received from all sides opera-texts, grave and gay, romantic and comic, great and small, but not one of these touched his heart. At length he was content " to keep quiet " and to wait, and only to sigh in secret for that unknown poet " who perhaps lives close by or in Timbuctoo —who knows ? " sighed he.

That, after the appearance of Jenny Lind, he kept in view her personality and gifts, is proved by his charming letters to Frau C.

Birch-Pfeiffer, in which, after different materials for Operas have been suggested to him,
from the Peasants' Wars and from Arnim's
"Kronenwächter," he urgently ·bespeaks a
Genoveva text. On this occasion his reverence for ancient traditions is clearly manifested ; for he requests the amiable poetess not
to remodel the charming old legend, and
would not have the action of the ancient fable
that still lives so vividly in the hearts of the
people disturbed, even for the sake of the
finest stage effects. He also rejected the
poetical death of Genoveva, suggested by his
friend. "It would certainly," said he, "be
much finer ; still I think it must not be, because contrary to the sense of the popular
tale." Unhappily, the fair saint was destined
to dissolve into vapor amid the solitude of the
forest, in spite of the many serious and pleasant
discussions that took place in the poet's little
study in 45 Leipziger Strasse, Berlin, while
the boughs of an ancient acacia tree tapped
inquisitively against the window, as if resolved
to hear something of what was going on.

However minutely they discussed the characters of the weak Count Palatine and the demoniacal Golo and all the interchange of ideas between the poetess and the musician, their joint and charming plan was never carried out, and remained a mere vision.

It was at that very time that Geibel, who was in Berlin, one evening after the performance of the "Midsummer Night's Dream," asked Mendelssohn why he had never written any greater Opera, and whether he intended to write one? Mendelssohn started up in excitement, and, looking at his friend with flashing eyes, exclaimed, "Give me a text that I can make use of, and I will get up at four o'clock to-morrow morning, and begin the composition."

"Well, then, what are your requirements for such a text?"

"Above all, it must have a definite purpose, and also be musical and thoroughly dramatic," was the answer. "In other respects I would not be too fastidious, and have no doubt I could adapt myself to any sphere. The 'Vestalin,' and ' Jessonda,' for instance, are good *libretti*. I should indeed infinitely prefer a popular German subject—of course not purely idyllic, but enlivened by strong and passionate conflicts. Fairy legends, too, would be acceptable under certain conditions. There is a peculiar charm when the personages in front of the stage act and sing, while in the background the elementary powers—woods, winds, and waters—have their say also."

These words of the musician fell like burning sparks on the poet's soul, and when Geibel quitted Berlin he had quite resolved to compose a libretto worthy of such a master. A summer passed in magic St. Goar on the Rhine produced the " Lorelei." But she did not appear as in the legend, an anomalous being between a demon and a fairy, but as a lovely simple mortal child, who, infatuated by love, sorrow, and revenge, falls a prey to the demoniac powers by her own act and deed, and is gradually transformed into the destructive enchantress of the legend. Thus a field for dramatic development was offered by this character. The design of the Opera was now lightly and gracefully constructed by the fancy of the poet; and when Geibel again met Mendelssohn in Berlin, in 1846, he could already sketch for him outlines of what the work was to be as a whole. Mendelssohn accepted the subject with lively satisfaction, and the leading conception exceedingly delighted him; although in some particulars, partly from musical grounds and also in the interest of the stage effect, he wished a great many alterations to be made. Regular meetings were arranged, and, eagerly exchanging ideas, they endeavored mutually to construct a new book. Mendelssohn signified in a general way his wishes and requirements, while the poet's eye and the poet's hand strove to shape a concrete form in accordance with them.

Unhappily, only a few weeks were granted them for this important work; and when the hour of parting came for the friends, not one-half of their task had been accomplished, and the closest correspondence could but faintly supply personal intercourse. How slowly in this way were wound up those minute discussions on the development of individual dramatic threads!—what an accumulation of scruples, suggestions, and counter-suggestions! Not till the ensuing spring were they so far in accord about the inner structure of the piece, that Geibel could commence its accomplishment in earnest. In order to be near the beloved master, and to work as much as possible in seclusion, Geibel first went to Altenburg, and thence to Dresden. From there he brought to him at Leipzig each act as it was finished. With heartfelt delight Mendelssohn saw the progress of the work, and always received the welcome poet with the utmost kindness. Their usual practice was to work together in the forenoon, to read and criticize what had been recently written, and then to stroll up and down the garden behind the house, dining in a happy family circle, and having music with their friends in the evening. David was sure to be there, inquiring playfully after " Fräulein Lorelei ; " Gade likewise asked about the fair enchantress ; Frau Livia

Frege sang; Frau von der Pfordten played; Jenny Lind, too, sometimes made her appearance, and in that lively circle the parts of the coming Opera were distributed.

But she, too, the bewitching "Lorelei," was not destined to emerge from the floods wrapped in the silvery vail of Mendelssohn's music; the glorious work remained a fragment; and deep sorrow steals over our hearts when we read this wondrously fine poem, which seems to gaze at us with eyes of the most profound melancholy, softly wailing, woe! woe!

Alas! it was but a short time that the indefatigable master was still to work and to create; the shades of that night "when no man can work" were gathering nearer and nearer. While all who loved and honored him believed so firmly and surely in a long life for the revered master, he himself forebodingly sang,

The rapid hours urge on the flight of spring.

Jenny Lind and Mendelssohn took leave of each other at Aix with the usual phrase—*Au revoir!*

He had resolved to direct his " Elijah " in Vienna, and Jenny Lind was to take the soprano part. With what delight and devotion did she study her glorious task, and with what joyous expectations did the composer himself look forward to the performance, preparations for which were being made on the grandest scale in Vienna! But never more on earth was he to hear that wondrous voice which had so often enchanted him!

Mendelssohn was detained from Leipzig in the spring of 1847, by journeys to various great musical festivals; he directed his " Elijah " in Birmingham, amid the most enthusiastic applause. There were four encores in the first part, and an equal number in the second; a vehement and unanimous call ensued for the composer at the close, and the audience showed a rapture of delight. And thus it was that this splendid Oratorio made its triumphal entrance into England.

A letter from Mendelssohn to his brother Paul describes the performance in his own lively and genial manner as follows :—

"From the very first you took so kind an interest in my 'Elijah,' and thus inspired me with so much energy and courage for its completion, that I must write to tell you of its first performance yesterday. No work of mine ever went so admirably the first time of execution, or was received with such enthusiasm by both the musicians and the audience, as the Oratorio. It was quite evident at the first rehearsal in London that they liked it, and liked to sing and to play it ; but I own I was far from anticipating that it would acquire such fresh vigor and impetus at the performance. Had you only been there. During the whole two hours and a half that it lasted, the two thousand people in the large hall, and the large orchestra, were all so fully intent on the one object in question, that not the slightest sound was to be heard among the whole audience, so that I could sway at pleasure the enormous orchestra and choir, and also the organ accompaniments. How often I thought of you during the time ! More especially, however, when the 'sound of abundance of rain' came, and

when they sang and played the final chorus
with *furore*, and when, after the close of the
first part, we were obliged to repeat the
whole movement. Not less than four choruses
and four airs were encored, and not one single
mistake occurred in the whole of the first part;
there were some afterward in the second part,
but even these were but trifling. A young
English tenor sang the last Air with such wonderful sweetness, that I was obliged to collect
all my energies not to be affected, and to continue beating time steadily. As I said before,
had you only been there!"

At this same music meeting, Mendelssohn
gave another of the numerous proofs of his
musical readiness. On one of the days of this
festival, an anthem of Händel's was to be performed. The concert had already fairly begun, when it was discovered that the recitative
which preceded the Coronation Anthem was
missing, but properly marked in the text-
books. One whispered the fact to another;
the musicians were in a state of alarm, the
directors of the festival in despair. They hur-

ried off to Mendelssohn, who was in an ante-
room, endeavoring to recover from the burden
and heat of the day, and lamented to him the
sudden and unforeseen difficulty. He tran-
quillized these excited individuals in his usual
amiable manner, desiring that writing materials and music-paper should be brought to
him at once; and in the course of half an hour
wrote out the recitative and the orchestral
parts. He found plenty of hands to transcribe
what he had written; the parts, still wet, were
distributed, and—the *prima vista* performance
was faultless.

A few days afterward, Mendelssohn directed
his "Elijah" in London, at Exeter Hall, with
equal success; and Prince Albert, that noble
patron and connoisseur of art, wrote the following words on the text-book he held in his hand
during the performance, and which he sent to
the composer:—

"To the noble artist who, though encompassed by the Baal-worship of false art, by his
genius and study has succeeded, like another
Elijah, in faithfully preserving the worship of

true art; once more habituating the ear, amid the giddy whirl of empty, frivolous sound, to the pure tones of sympathetic feeling and legitimate harmony;—to the great master who, by the tranquil current of his thoughts, reveals to us the gentle whisperings, as well as the mighty strife of the elements,—to him is this written in grateful remembrance, by

" ALBERT."

"Buckingham Palace."

It is well known how highly the Queen of England esteemed the German composer, and how graciously she treated him. She received him in her most intimate circle, and caused her pet birds to be carried out of the music-room to prevent their singing while Mendelssohn was playing. She requested him, in the most amiable manner, to play some of his own compositions, and herself sang some of his songs. With an engaging smile, she expressed her dissatisfaction with her own performance, appealing playfully to her teacher, Lablache, who, she said, could vouch for her sometimes singing very tolerably; but she felt timid before him—the composer of all those beautiful things. While Mendelssohn was playing, she sat beside him at the piano, watching his hands. He played a great deal on that evening, in the music-room of the august lady, and writes to his mother that it was a delight to play all that "the pretty and most charming Queen Victoria wished to hear, who looks so youthful, and is so gently courteous and gracious, who speaks such good German, and knows all my music so well." She was never weary of asking, so he played seven of his "Songs without Words" and the Serenade, and concluded by twice extemporizing.

After the first performance of the "Elijah," Mendelssohn returned to Leipzig, and writes that he had been obliged to remodel some passages in the "Elijah" that had given him no small trouble. He was harassed, too, at that time, by anxiety about a faithful old servant—a fresh proof of his warm heart. The worthy Johann, who had accompanied him on his Swiss journey, and was so beloved by the children, was now prostrated by mortal sick-

ness; and it is touching to read in his letter:
" I am often, too, in no happy mood, for poor
Johann is very seriously ill, and causes us
really very great anxiety. ' May I be so bold
as to ask who is to play the part of the servant?' says Göthe, and lately these words often
recurred to me. May God soon restore the
poor faithful fellow!" But the attached Johann died, deeply lamented by his master, for
whom he left a letter and his last will, of which
Mendelssohn writes to Klingemann, "I must
show you this the next time we meet. No
man, no poet indeed, could have written anything more heartfelt, earnest, and touching."

CHAPTER VIII.

Sail on ! sail on ! 'tis not for me
To question where the port may be !

MENDELSSOHN, when traveling, was ever like
a merry bird escaped from his cage, who
spreads his wings and enjoys his golden freedom. He was thoroughly imbued with the
truth of the poet's words :—

Whom God would bless for evermore,
He casteth on Life's stormy shore;

and he saw and enjoyed everything that was
to be seen, in all its fullness and with clear perceptions. In addition to every other gift, he
possessed that invaluable one—to see all things
with an eye of love. His letters, while traveling in Italy and Switzerland, sufficiently prove
this, and at Frankfort he was always as gay as
a child. Paris alone he seems to have found
less sympathetic, and we learn from these letters that he never stayed long there. One day
he left Paris for Aix, where he was expected.

7*

When at the small frontier station of Herbesthal, the passport of the traveler was demanded. He had no passport. "I am Mendelssohn," was his simple answer to the indignant inspector of passports, who stalked up to him in all the consciousness of his rights. "Mendelssohn!" repeated the executor of the law, "I am no wiser than I was before. I demand your passport." "Well, I am Kapell-meister Mendelssohn, or I may say General Music - Director of the King of Prussia." "Any one can say that! you must remain here." No remonstrances availed; the Herr General Music-Director was actually forced to stay in Herbesthal, and on a very dismal rainy day too, as an eye-witness of the incident relates. Telegraph-posts were not yet erected in those days, so Mendelssohn was obliged to content himself by intrusting the guard of the train with a few lines to a friend in Aix, begging him to repair to Herbesthal with all speed for the purpose of identifying and releasing a captive musician. Meanwhile he took up his quarters patiently in the best inn in the small town, which he found to be a most melancholy asylum, with red-flowered curtains, and a desolate room filled with the odor of stale tobacco. The boots and the girl of the inn looked with astonishment at the well-bred guest without any luggage, who was so quiet, and did not seem to think it necessary to proclaim his presence to the whole house by incessant ringing of bells. A long time must still elapse before the arrival of the next train. The rain pattered down unremittingly; and even in fine weather the market-place of Herbesthal is by no means so interesting an object as the Linden-Allée in Berlin. The drops trickled noiselessly to the ground through the foliage of an old chestnut-tree before the house, collecting in a dark pool, which seemed to form an object of the most lively interest to geese, dogs, and children by turns, judging from their different modes of endeavoring to fathom its depth; on the opposite side of the way, before the smithy, stood a weary-looking, worn-out old horse, allowing the rain to pour down on him with a patience worthy of admiration, and not attempting to stir; at intervals a maid in *sabots* clattered by, her dress tucked up; or a wagoner in a blue smock-frock floundered past. Such was the view from the inn window which that day rejoiced the eyes of the composer of "St. Paul" at Herbesthal.

Suddenly, from a short distance, the sounds of an old piano were heard, the notes feeble but in tune, and a charming girlish voice began to sing, "On song's bright pinions." What mattered now the rainy day and all Herbesthal? This was *sunshine*, filling the miserable little room with brightness and warmth. The banks of the Ganges river loomed before him, where, as Heinrich Heine in that song tells us, gentle and innocent gazelles lightly bound, where violets nestle and peep at the stars, and where roses whisper soft love-tales. The youthful singer had indeed little idea of *who* was thus borne aloft on the "'bright pinions' of *her* song."

Whether she is still living, I know not, but I should like to have heard from herself, her feelings, when the composer of the beautiful air thanked her courteously for her simple, charming singing, and when his friends arrived from Aix to fetch him in triumph and to carry him off with them, and finally when he sat down at the shabby old piano, and, as a farewell, in presence of the whole astonished family, extemporized on the theme, " On song's bright pinions." Without, the rain still poured down ; but the fair young daughter of the innkeeper, who had retreated shyly into a recess of the window, her eyes steadily fixed on the player, must have seen bright blue sky above her ; and in the aftercourse of every - day life, amid Heaven knows what cares and sorrows, when she recalls that day, surely she must once more see a bit of bright azure sky overhead.

Mendelssohn appears to have been always particularly happy in England, and his letters are full of sunny reminiscences of that island so beloved by him. Mendelssohn's friendship with Klingemann in London, like all the most heartfelt ties of the kind, first took root in the days of their youth, when Klingemann was very intimate with Mendelssohn's family in Berlin.

Ferdinand Hiller's attractive pen has furnished an eloquent memorial to this noble artistic nature in a charming book of his, recently published, " Aus dem Tonleben unserer Zeit." His article on the death of Klingemann appeared in the " Kölnischer Zeitung " immediately after his death—Sept. 25, 1862. " The deceased," writes Hiller, " belonged to that thinly-sown, chosen order of men, who assume a prominent place in society, and combine the most refined and solid culture, nobility of thought, and self-sacrificing amiability in social life, with the most productive talent."

I myself recently saw a portrait of Klingemann, taken from that by Professor Hensel— a most striking and intellectual head, with genuine poet's eyes, and a grand forehead.

Karl Klingemann was Secretary to the Hanoverian Embassy in Berlin till 1821, when he went to London to fill a similar position for more than thirty years. His poetical soul, his enthusiasm for music, as well as his profound knowledge of that art, gave rise to a fervent friendship between him and Mendelssohn—a bright bond only severed by death. From first to last, Mendelssohn attached the highest value to Klingemann's judgment, and the correspondence of the two devoted friends is a treasure that still rests in the hands of his widow. From the year 1828, to 1847, 154 letters are deposited in the shrine of relics belonging to the amiable bereaved Frau Sophie Klingemann, whose heart finds its sole consolation in the memories of a happy past, in all its rare beauty and harmony. What a casket of gems! In addition to these precious letters are some enchanting poems, many of which are on all lips, through the medium of Mendelssohn's music. Books of songs composed by Klingemann, and the poetry also partly written by him, were published by Breitkopf & Härtel. We find also the most beautiful pencil sketches by the hand of Mendelssohn, and, as a curiosity, a gigantic letter of thanks, written on a huge sheet of paper by each member of the Mendelssohn family (with the exception of Paul), immediately after the performance of the Operetta "Die Heimkehr aus der Fremde," the poetry of which was written by Klingemann, and the music by Felix, in honor of the "silver wedding-day" of his parents. One after another, notable hands, large and small, are sketched uplifted in gratitude to narrate and describe. Felix leads the way with a motto taken from the Operetta—

Lieschen was a charming child,
And never told a lie.

Then the mother writes in her wonderfully clear correct characters, succeeded by Fanny and Rebecca, and finally by the father, and Felix writes the conclusion. All those hands now rest for ever, and he to whom this precious letter was addressed, rests also, while the poor fragile paper lies before my eyes uninjured, destined to survive so much excellence. Karl Klingemann formed one of the audience at Düsseldorf at the first performance of "St. Paul" there, and wrote at the time an enthusiastic letter in English to a friend of his in London, Mr. Horsley, to whose house he at once brought Mendelssohn when he came to

England. It was in the year 1829 that the two friends undertook that interesting journey to the Highlands of Scotland that gave rise to the most charming diary that perhaps was ever kept by two pilgrims. Mendelssohn sketched the different points of view, and Klingemann wrote three poetical illustrations on the margin of the leaves.

The first sketch represents the bachelor quarters of the London Hanoverian Secretary, Karl Klingemann, on the evening before the journey. It is quite a chequered scene. Open traveling-bags lie scattered about on chairs and on the floor, while the tables are strewn with various toilet appliances, intermixed with books, maps, and provisions—among the latter of which a large Cheshire cheese and a bottle of porter are conspicuous. In the midst of this chaos stands a vase of flowers most charmingly poetical. The window stands wide open and beyond the roofs of houses and past high steeples, the view is lost in the blue distance. Klingemann wrote as follows:

"June 27, 1829.

> Here is the Present—all our own!
>   And yet she cometh strangely vailed,
>   As though her wonted courage failed—
> As if unwilling to be known.
>
> The Present like the Future seems—
>   That dread uncalculated sum—
>   And things in distant years to come
> Are looming through the spring sunbeams."

And now for the journey itself. The most inimitable humor, combined with the most profound earnestness; all sorts of amusing adventures on rainy days in wretched inns; water-parties with *obbligato* chattering of teeth, and admiration in turn of the splendors of nature on so wild and grand a scale, as well as of the structures of men's hands, ivy-covered abbeys, and ancient cathedrals. One page with a sketch of Edinburgh and its watery girdle is of such vast beauty that I could scarcely turn my eyes from it.

In after years the slightest reminiscence of this Scotch tour awakened the most sunny cheerfulness in Mendelssohn's heart, while Klingemann also to the day of his death invariably alluded with the most grateful delight to this true and genuine "spring-time."

Mendelssohn quickly found himself at home with the Horsley family in London. There he met with the true comfort of an English gentleman's family; and it is well known that Mendelssohn was very susceptible to the charm of a well-regulated household, like that of his parental home. Three charming daughters glided like the Graces through the elegant rooms—Mary, Fanny, and Sophy. The heart of the youthful German musician must have beat with excitement in the constant presence and familiar conversation of these fascinating creatures, so highly gifted and carefully educated, and full of enthusiasm for the marvelous genius of Mendelssohn. Felix always called the eldest daughter, for whom he had the most lively admiration, "the lovely Mary," and report says she was a truly regal-looking beauty. Subsequently she married the celebrated engineer Brunel. Fanny, who became Mrs. Thomson, and, after a few short years of conjugal happiness, sank into the grave, appeared almost insignificant beside her more brilliant sister, like the lily of the valley beside the rose; but her sweet face, her intellect and grace, attracted every visitor in her father's house; while the youngest, at that time almost a child, exhibited extraordinary musical endowments, in the cultivation of which Mendelssohn took the warmest interest. How many a dear German friend Mendelssohn introduced by letter to this hospitable family; and in the year 1844, Klingemann presented to them a youth, whom Mendelssohn had sent to him, with the following letter:—

BERLIN, March 10, 1844.

"MY BELOVED FRIEND: I wish to make you acquainted by these lines with a lad who, during the three-quarters of a year that I have known him, has become very dear to my heart, and who has gained my love and high esteem to a degree that I may say I have latterly experienced for very few. His name is *Joseph Joachim*, a boy of thirteen years of age, from Pesth, in Hungary. He intends to pay a visit of some months to his uncle Figdor, a London merchant. I cannot say enough to you of his truly wonderful talent for the violin. You must first, however, hear him yourself, and the manner in which he can play all possible solos, both of the past and the present, and decipher and interpret every kind of music, in order to place him as high as I do, and to anticipate the glorious results which must accrue to art through him. He is, moreover, sound at heart, an admirable, well-educated, thoroughly genuine, shrewd lad, of great good sense, and the strictest integrity. Be kind, therefore, to him; take some charge of him in great London, and present him to those of our acquaintances who know how to appreciate such glorious talent as his, and from whom he can in turn derive pleasure and improvement. I here allude principally to the Horsleys. Take him to Chorley's, also, if you can, and, above all, remember that any kindness you show to him, you show also to me. May we soon, God willing, have a happy meeting! When spring arrives, I hope also to come to you.

"Your Felix."

It was during a visit to the Horsleys, in the year 1846, that a charming German girl, So-

phie Rosen, from Detmold, (afterward Klingemann's wife), first saw Felix Mendelssohn, and
received that powerful conviction of that noble
artist's impressible and impressive personality,
which so many hearts had previously experienced, and which so many were still to experience.   He addressed her with all the magic
charm of his graceful courtesy, for her brother,
the intellectual Orientalist, Friedrich Rosen,
was one of the most intimate London friends
both of Klingemann and Mendelssohn.   They
were called the German *trefoil*, so constantly
were they to be seen together; and how gay,
yet how grave, were they when together!   At
one moment, in the most eager excitement,
poring over all sorts of strange old Indian
MSS., which the young scholar deciphered and
explained to his friends, or plunged deep into
discussions about life and art, immortality and
music; and in the next, jesting and laughing
like children.

One day Felix and Klingemann left a highly
original invitation at Rosen's house, on not
finding him at home, asking him to dinner on

the following day. The large page is written double—that is, Mendelssohn wrote one line, Klingemann the next, and so on, only the writing of the one was to be read from the top to the bottom of the page, and the other the reverse way; while the one appears quite legible, the other stands on its head, and *vice versa*, each going its own way, so that it is quite a piece of labor to decipher the page filled with the most brilliant wit. The close of the page is, " Do come—be hungry, agreeable, and yourself." At the end is the following notice, " Tournez, s'il vous *pleut*," with a neatly executed sketch of a spread umbrella. The whole is carefully placed in an envelop, addressed and marked as " *A valuable Indian Manuscript.*"

When, in 1845, Klingemann and his young wife first opened their hospitable rooms in Hobart Place, Eaton Square, Mendelssohn was one of their first guests, and nothing can be more charming than to hear Frau Sophie Klingemann speak of his engaging amiability and cheerfulness. A very attractive sister of hers was at that time on a visit to them, and in their letters to their parents neither could say enough about their beloved and joyous guest, who evidently felt himself quite at home with them. Mendelssohn, however, was already so celebrated, that visits and invitations overwhelmed him in the most remarkable manner during his stay, so their confidential evenings would have been few in number, but for a stratagem to which they resorted—to say that none of the family were at home. On these occasions, they sat in the drawing-room with the curtains drawn and the lamp shaded, and talked, and sketched, and made verses, while carriages outside drove up, and the knocking and inquiries for Mr. Mendelssohn were endless, each receiving the same disappointing answer, " not at home," while within they laughed and rejoiced *con sordini* as each intruder was dispatched. Not till the hour for visitors was passed, did they venture to open the piano.

Madame Klingemann and her sister had been educated at home by their father, and among other things had studied Latin with him, and particularly the Odes of Sorace. It was, therefore, a source of peculiar pleasure to their renowned guest to test the acquirements of the charming sisters, and he expressed the utmost delight when the examination passed without any stumbling-blocks, and he was enabled to award them a *first-class* certificate. He often quoted a passage in the middle of some ode to them—when, to his astonishment and delight, the rest of the passage was always forthcoming. Klingemann would sit beside them with his shrewd smile, enjoying the pleasure of his wife and sister, as well as that of his friend. Meanwhile Felix sometimes suddenly started up, and sat down at the piano to play some theme that occurred to him at the moment, when he would summon Klingemann to his side, and both in a second became absorbed in a discussion on music, while the fair young wife listened with the expression that seems to say,

When wisdom speaks, I gladly lend an ear,
Because I may believe the words I hear;

8

and the graceful Marie glided about noiselessly, arranging the tea-table, till some sudden inspiration of Mendelssohn's fancy collected them all round him in silent and enthusiastic admiration.

The same small circle often assembled at
the Thomsons' and Horsleys', and a charming
sketch of Mendelssohn's, now in the possession
of Frau Sophie Klingemann, represents a tea-
table at Fanny Thomson's, round which all
those lovely young women are seated, and the
two friends.

Occasionally the society was enlarged by
that ever-welcome couple, the Moscheles.
Benedict came with his handsome wife, a
lively dark-eyed Neapolitan; Bennett and
his young wife, Chorley, etc., or the same
party met in one of the hospitable houses I
have named. There every one, according to
their own inclinations, either conversed with
ease and unrestraint, or enjoyed music, and
even the pencil was not always at rest. How
many a sketch was retained by fair hands as
the sole memorial of those happy days! Men-

delssohn was composing at that time a Strophe in the album of Frau Klingemann, with the intention of adding a fresh part at each visit. "The thing must have at least sixteen parts," said he.

However brilliant Mendelssohn appeared in larger evening parties, his innate overflowing gay spirits, the charm of which was said to be quite irresistible,.were only known to his most intimate friends. On his first visit after Klingemann's marriage, he bespoke from the bride his favorite dish for dinner next day, honest English roast beef, humbly begging also for a cherry pie, with custards. When his friend asked him about the incidents on his journey, he answered with a merry smile, "Except sea-sickness, I met with nothing new, only it did seem strange to me to meet so many English on the road." · "Oh! that old joke; have you not yet forgotten it?" said Klingemann laughing, and they immediately plunged into merry remembrances of their Highland journey, during which they had met "such a remarkable number of Scotch people!"

On that evening the friends agreed to a *partie quarrée* to Blackwall, to enjoy one of the fish dinners for which it was celebrated, and which Mendelssohn already knew and liked much. Indeed, at no time does he seem to have been insensible to the excellences of the English *cuisine*. It was a joyous expedition, and a joyous meal in a little pavilion close to the river, the blue watery expanse lying spread out before their gay and admiring eyes, placid and rippling in the light of the evening sun. And besides this charming object, there were newly-caught, capital fish, good wine, lovely, blooming, female faces, the familiar German tones in a foreign land, and jovial toasts, rhymed and unrhymed! Never, perhaps, was a merrier fish dinner than on that day in the little pavilion, decorated with mussel-shells, by the water-side.

How truly his attached London friends sympathized in all his German and English triumphs, when first his "St. Paul," and afterward the "Elijah," was so enthusiastically received in England; when Mendelssohn's songs and Mendelssohn's compositions were sung and played in every musical house, and above all in the salon of "the gracious Queen!" While all this delight and appreciation by those so dear to him was ever most highly valued of all by the heart of the renowned master, who never for one moment was divested of the wonderful modesty of true genius, which always regards itself as merely on the path that leads to the highest goal, but never thinks that it is already attained, gratefully accepting every counsel, every opinion, every interchange of ideas. To this the survivors can testify with the deepest reverence and emotion. And after the most brilliant fêtes and honors, how happy he invariably seemed at the modest tea-tables of his friends, where, instead of a laurel crown, a simple nosegay, gathered by fair hands, adorned the place of the beloved guest. In the hearts of all those fortunate beings who enjoyed the privilege of his intimacy, Felix has left the same ineffaceable image — the image of an incomparably noble and harmonious nature, both as a man and as an artist.

In May, 1847, Klingemann and his wife accompanied Mendelssohn to Calais, on their way to the Continent. It was on this very journey that the tidings of Fanny's death was to reach him. Mendelssohn had offered to escort Madame Klingemann to Germany as far as Cologne, where her own relations were to receive her, while he himself was to proceed to Frankfort, where Cécile and the children eagerly expected him. He suffered very much in crossing, which, indeed, he never bore well; so that Klingemann, who on the evening previous to the journey from London had been seized by an inexplicable feeling of uneasiness, resolved to go part of the way with him, and to escort his beloved companions as far as Ostend. They had hired a carriage in Calais, and now traveled in all possible comfort; and during this delightful tour, favored by the most splendid weather, Mendelssohn soon recovered, and was restored to his usual cheerfulness. In the reminiscences of Madame Klingemann, those days of travel seem to have been a mixture of sky-blu,e sunny gold, snow-white blossoms, and luminous seas. It was the *last* time that those devotedly attached friends were to be together. The hour of parting came; they shook hands with the consolatory last words on their lips, "to meet again." But confidently as these words of hope and farewell were spoken on both sides, tears were in their eyes, and their hearts were strangely depressed, as if from a presentiment that—*never* were they to meet again! It was possibly at that time that Klingemann wrote the pleasing poem which now rests in Frau Sophie's casket of relics:

A FAREWELL.

Wandering bird of passage,
　Thou fain wouldst fly away!
But there's a thread of magic
　Compelling.thee to stay.

A slender thread of magic,
　And yet a potent spell,
Will bind the bird of passage
　To those who love him well.

Faint strains of fairy music
　That sound so far away!
Ye are the morning heralds
　That harbinger the day.

And as the Alpine ridges
　Shine radiant to the last,
Ye are the distant echoes
　Of the glories of the past.

The last flickering of Mendelssohn's usual gay spirits when on a journey, the animated mood inspired by travel, is described by Ferdinand von W——, in a letter to his friend Frau Malwine B. S——. The following was written *after* Mendelssohn's death :—

" Who would not feel awe-struck when death thus mows down? What an affliction, the death of Mendelssohn! Again and again I exclaim! It is impossible! How I rejoiced when only one short month ago he came to Freiburg, for the first time since Fanny's death more lively and cheerful! How I strove to promote this! He was the noblest man I ever knew. I always felt elevated and excited in his presence, and so much gratified by his liking for myself. One day we were in Badenweiler together, in lovely weather. I now constantly recall that expedition. How charming he was on that day—and how he talked! All that he said was so delightful, and so refined, though even his playfulness was tinged with gravity. We were on the summit of the tower, and when we began to descend, I suddenly shouted to him behind me to catch me if he could. We then ran down the winding stair, at the risk of a tumble; but, in spite of the start I had, I could scarcely arrive first; and when we were below, how he laughed in his old way, and, laying hold of me, said, in the joyous tone of former days, " We are two children!" He could run like the wind, and enjoyed doing so. The real grandeur of his creations—how will they now be doubly acknowledged! His is an everlasting name, and a life of fame is a long one. Ah! would that he could ever be equaled! And with so much fame, how much *love* was also bestowed on him! And now he lies sleeping in the grave —our inimitable Felix!"

The journey to Switzerland, alluded to in this letter, was to be his last here below. No other gay pilgrimage was destined for him on this beautiful earth; the journey was drawing to *a close.*

CHAPTER IX.

It is enough.   O Lord receive my soul.
—*Mendelssohn's " St. Paul."*

AFTER the concert, where Reichardt's ". Violet " song won so many friends, I took leave of Mendelssohn, in order to reside for some time in Berlin.

" Be sure to call on my sister, Fanny Hensel," said he; " she has heard much good of you. Sing and practice assiduously, and think often of me! Next winter you will come forward in very different form—and that will be a joyful day ! "

And with touching kindness did Frau Fanny Hensel receive the timid young girl, when she paid her first visit. How distinctly do I still see before me the long bright room in which she welcomed me! She rose from the piano as I came in, with outstretched hand. Frau Rebecca Dirichlet and Herr von Kendell were with her. Fanny Hensel was little, a brunette, and her gestures animated, while her deep dark eyes seemed to look into your very heart. Rebecca I recollect as slender and pale, her delicate features bearing more resemblance to those of her brother. And now I had to tell them all about Felix. How gladly I did so! So we soon fell into the most easy strain of conversation. Fran Hensel then gave me, in the most amiable manner, a general invitation to her celebrated Sunday *matinées.*

What a store of delightful and rich enjoyment I reaped in that house! In what a gloriously golden light do those days in Berlin still seem to float before my memory! I heard that genuine artist Fanny play, and was privileged to sing Mendelssohn's songs to her.

A variety of forms flitted past me, and my youthful soul received powerful and ineffaceable impressions of the most varied nature. Many a noble image, many a sweet sound and tone still rest among the sacred relics I treasure in my memory. I can never forget the wonderful playing also of Herr von Keudell, now Secretary of Legation and the friend of Count Bismarck, and who was an almost daily guest at that time of the Hensels.

One *matinée*, in particular, I can still recall as vividly as if I had only yesterday been present at it. A circle of elegant ladies; a throng of gentlemen with stars and without; the fascinating Pauline von Schätzel-Decker; a pretty young pianist from Schleswig, Toni Tiedemann; Auguste Löwe, a contralto, and her sweet sister, Georgine; the Mesdames Türrschmidt; the musicians, Gans, Taubert, and Rungenhagen; Professor Hensel himself; Paul Mendelssohn, Professor Dirichlet, the imposing figures of Herr von Kendell, Richard Wuerst, and others. One female form on that day more especially excited my highest interest, from which I really could not turn away my eyes. It was that of Henriette Sontag, Countess Rossi, in violet silk and a crimson shawl equally aristocratic and bewitching. And on that morning, in the presence of all these grandees, known and unknown, the little Leipzig girl was to sing Men-

delssohn's " Reiselied," accompanied by Fanny
Hensel—

Convey the greetings of my faithful heart !

and she thought of *him* whose warm introduction she would not for the world have disgraced,
and carolled fresh and free, like the birds in
the forest, and Frau Fanny smiled and nodded,
and whispered, " Felix ought to have heard
that!" and Henriette Sontag said a few good-
natured words to the young singer, and looked
at her so kindly with her deep blue eyes, and
so much charming music ensued, that " the
little one " went home quite intoxicated with
delight.

A small sheet of pale blue paper lies at this
moment before me, on which a graceful hand,
in beautiful penmanship, had written as follows :—

" *To Fräulein Lili Vogel.*

" My Dear Fräulein: I have been unfortunately obliged to postpone my next musical
matinée till Sunday week, but I trust this may
not deprive me of the pleasure of seeing you.

Meanwhile, I have fixed to-morrow at five o'clock for my rehearsal. If there is nothing to prevent it, I beg you to come for a little; we can then have some music together for our own amusement, and, if the weather clears up, sing some four-part songs in the garden.

"Yours,   FANNY HENSEL."

In the month of May, only a few weeks after those enchanting quartettes in the open air, Fanny Hensel was dead! Felix Mendelssohn was right when he wrote, "No one who once knew my sister can *ever* forget her through life!"

In the meantime the concert season in Leipzig had come to a close. On March 11, 1847, Mendelssohn directed the last subscription concert, where Robert Schumann's new Symphony in C major was performed. Shortly after, he conducted a concert of Clara Schumann's, where that enchantress played his G minor Concerto in the most exquisite manner. During this time he was occupied in the most heterogeneous works—his "Lorelei," and his Oratorio of "Christus," various Motetts, and a Scherzo for stringed instruments. His health, however, to the extreme alarm of his family, had become very fluctuating, amid all these varied and unremitting labors, and he complained much of headaches and weariness. After giving a performance of his " St. Paul " on Good Friday, Mendelssohn, contrary to the advice of his physicians, proceeded to encounter new toils of every kind in London, where the " Elijah " had been given three consecutive times, with ever increasing enthusiasm. He likewise went to Manchester to direct his " Elijah," and, on May 11, played, for the last time in public, at a Court concert in London, Beethoven's G major Concerto, with the most splendid extemporized cadences, and directed the music of his " Midsummer Night's Dream."

After all these exertions and triumphs he felt an irresistible longing for a quiet retired life; he yearned for a meeting with his brother and sisters, and for a thorough *dolce far niente.*

A grand family meeting was arranged by him, when in London, at beautiful Frankfort, where Mendelssohn had found his happiness; and there, by the side of his beloved wife, in the circle of his children, like a flash of lightning in a serene sky, the dreadful tidings reached him of Fanny's death! Let us draw a vail over this sacred sorrow!

The list of his compositions in 1847 is as follows:—

1847.

Three Motetts for Chorus and Solo Voices. Baden-Baden and Leipzig.

Recitative and Choruses from the unfinished Oratorio, " Christus."

Finale of the first Act from the unfinished Opera of " Lorelei."

Quartette for two Violins, Tenor, and Violoncello, in F minor. Andante and Scherzo for two Violins, Tenor, and Violoncello, in op. 81.

Songs for One Voice with Pianoforte.

Song for Four Male Voices.

Song for Two Voices with Pianoforte, " Das Aehrenfeld."

Song for Voice with Pianoforte, " Altdeutsches Frühlingslied:"

> Gloomy winter is no more,
> The swallows through the welkin soar.

Mendelssohn's last composition, written on October 7, 1847, in Leipzig.

Mendelssohn quitted Frankfort with his family, to spend the summer in Interlaken; Paul Mendelssohn and his wife and Professor Hensel accompanied them.

He took refuge with his loved ones and his grief in the stupendous Alpine world, and there the mourners lived together in seclusion, and, as it were, hand in hand, *in memoriam* of the lost one who could no longer be among them ; and it was the sweet balm of holy nature, and the magic of childish eyes, that extracted the sharpest thorns from their too just grief, and gradually consoled Mendelssohn's bruised heart. Though bowed down with sorrow, he occupied himself incessantly with his children. At length his well-beloved brother and sister returned home, although on this occasion the separation was inexpressibly hard to bear. He felt always better in the open air. He took long rambles with his children, and also wandered about alone, when no doubt he felt the truth of the lines in one of his own sweetest "Spring Songs,"

Sorrow melts like soft dissolving snow.

8*

And never was heart more susceptible than his to the charms of God's beautiful world. He has sung the splendors of every season of the year; and no one felt more deeply than he did the sweet consolations of spring—from the "first violet" to that *last* sad

Sweet spring, thou art departed.

No one ever had a more genuine love of roses—

Now roses bloom;

or delighted more in the autumn—

Withered leaves rustle in the woods,

where the fair one lingers in the

Bright world of bloom.

Winter alone calls forth a lament:

So small the earth, we hardly know
To what poor hut or hole to go,
From blinding sleet, or driving snow;

and indeed, it was *winter* that hurried him into the smallest and narrowest of all huts— the grave.

During his last stay in Interlaken, Mendelssohn withdrew from all society; strangers were intolerable to him. His grief drove him into solitude, for every great and true grief must isolate us; the fewer sounds that reached him from the world without, the more beneficial was it to him. We can realize a very touching picture of his secluded life there from various passages in his letters of that date.

"Since the day before yesterday it has been quite cold besides, so we have a fire in-doors, and out-of-doors streaming rain. But I cannot deny that I sometimes rather like such downright pouring wet days, which confine you effectually to the house. This time they give me an opportunity of passing the whole day with my three elder children ; they write, and learn arithmetic and Latin with me—paint landscapes during their play-hours, or play draughts, and ask a thousand wise questions, which no fool can answer (people generally say the reverse of this, still it is so). The standing reply is, and always will be, ' You do not yet understand such things,' which still vibrates in my ears from my own mother, and which I shall soon hear in turn from my children, when they give their children the same answer ; and thus it goes on."

In another letter to Paul Mendelssohn he says :—

"I have begun to write music very busily; the three elder children work with me in the forenoon; in the afternoon, when the weather permits, we all take a walk together; and I have also finished a few rabid sketches in Indian ink."

And finally:

" My wife and children are well, God be praised ! We walk a great deal, the children do their lessons, Cécile paints Alpine roses, and I write music; so the days•pass monotonously and quickly."

How distinctly do we thus picture to ourselves the scene as actually before us—the spacious room with the fire-place, and through the open door of the balcony a view of the inimitable Jungfrau in all her crystal beauty ! A circle of blooming children round the table, their rosy faces bent over the pages of different books, yet laughing and chatting at intervals. Lili on a footstool with her doll, little Felix playing on the floor near his mother. At a

small table in the full light sits the lovely
Cécile, her golden-brown curls drooping over
her delicate cheeks; in front of her stands a
vase filled with rhododendrons, while her fragile hand rests on the leaves of an album, in
which those Alpine roses have just been
sketched. Her long eyelashes are raised from
time to time, and those matchless eyes seek
one alone with the loving tenderness of a devoted wife. And Felix looks paler and thinner
than formerly, with a dreamy absent air gazing away from the music-paper into the far
distance—the pen has escaped from his hand.
Whither are his thoughts straying? Possibly
it may be the melody of his wonderful " Nachtlied " that at this moment hovers before his
soul :

Now shines out the evening star,
And chime of bells comes from afar.

His return to Leipzig, and his first meeting
with his faithful friends, after the death of her
who could never be forgotten, agitated Mendelssohn beyond all measure. The wound,
scarcely yet cicatrized, was now once more violently torn open. In spite of the wish that

every one showed to spare his feelings, still
some allusion to the fatal event was inevitable,
and hence it was that he so repeatedly declared,
" The air of Leipzig stifles me ; it is so oppressive everywhere ! " He went to Berlin for a
short time, and only returned to Leipzig to
prepare for a journey to Vienna, whither he
had promised to go to conduct his " Elijah."
He resumed his labors with eager haste and
burning zeal, in spite of constantly recurring
pains in his head, and attacks of faintness ; and
to Cécile's tender entreaties to spare himself,
he only replied, " Let me work on—for me too
the hour of rest will come ! " and to those
friends who assailed him with similar remonstrances, he replied in a determined manner,
" Let me work while it is yet day. Who can
tell how soon the bell may toll ? "

Mendelssohn always composed in his head,
and never at the piano. Like Mozart, every
piece of music, with all its instrumentation,
was in his mind before he wrote it down.
Sometimes an idea occurred to him when
seated at the piano, which he then hastily

noted down, and subsequently resumed and worked out in his head. A comparison with our glorious Mozart suggests itself forcibly in many phases of Mendelssohn's being, both as a man and as an artist; above all, in the prodigious power of work and activity of his equally brief artistic career. He had likewise the same childlike enjoyment of life, and was equally absorbed in his beloved art. Mendelssohn's *unpublished* works are scarcely fewer in number than those published.

On the 7th October, 1847, Mendelssohn composed that sweet, profoundly melancholy "Spring Song," the last verse of which runs thus:—

> Idol of my inmost heart!
> Life for me is endless sorrow—
> Blackest night without a morrow—
> For thou and I must part.

He then pushed aside the still wet page, and starting up, said hastily, "Enough! Don't be uneasy, Cécile, any longer; I really mean to write no more, and to rest awhile!"

Two days afterward Mendelssohn brought his newest book of songs to his musical friend, Frau Livia Frege, who was in the habit of seeing him so often come into her house with a score under his arm, and singing the half-finished piece to him at sight. On this occasion she was to sing for him, with her sweet voice, the "Nachtlied." They first tried over some portions of "St. Paul," and different songs. Mendelssohn's excessive nervous irritability had for some time past been very striking, whether in listening to music or in playing himself. His face changed, and he became very pale. Indeed, he avoided all large musical gatherings, and repeatedly declared that "the highest delight, and the highest of all enjoyments, is in reality music among a few friends—at most, a quartette of congenial spirits. At present I care for nothing beyond this."

On the day in question, Mendelssohn had played a great deal the same morning with Moscheles and David, and to his anxious friend, Madame L. Frege, he appeared weary and exhausted. When at last she sang the following lines—

Time marches on by night as well as day,
And many march by night who fain would stay,

Mendelssohn said, with a shudder, "Oh! that has a dreary sound, but it is just what I feel!" He then suddenly rose, as pale as death, and paced the room hurriedly, complaining that his hands were as cold as ice. To Frau Livia Frege's anxious and earnest entreaty to drive straight home and send for a doctor, he answered with a smile, that a good quick walk would be of greater service to him, and took leave of her. He, however, gave up his intention of taking a walk, and went straight home; but in the evening he was similarly affected, and obliged to remain in bed for some days. This attack of debility seemed to have passed away, and Mendelssohn again received visits from his intimate friends; indeed, on October 28th, he took a short walk with his wife, and was tolerably well and in good spirits at dinner. In the afternoon, to the consternation of his family, he was seized with a sudden, deep swoon.

The physician could not dissemble his alarm at this attack of illness; his state was soon hopeless, for a paralytic stroke ensued. Mendelssohn lay for a long time insensible; and when he once more recovered consciousness, he continued in an apathetic state, only complaining at intervals of insupportable pains in his head. In this condition he continued for seven days, with little change for better or worse—days full of torment and mortal anguish to all who loved him.

The intelligence of the danger that threatened this precious life spread like wildfire through the city; it was as if some beloved king had been in peril of his life; crowds of anxious inquirers besieged the well-known house in the Königsstrasse, anxiously hoping for a better report. On every side were seen sorrowing faces and sympathizing inquirers.

And within, in the darkened sick-room, the mortal frame of one of the noblest of men was undergoing the last great struggle, surrounded by faithful friends, in the arms of inconsolable but self-sacrificing love; and, at nine o'clock at night, on the 4th November, 1847, the hand of the Angel of Death wrote underneath the Book of Life of him who had gone to his rest his hallowed *Fine.*

The purest of artistic souls had returned to the Source of Light, whence it emanated.

Deeply affecting were the marks of respect shown to the mortal remains of Mendelssohn by the city for whose musical life he had labored so efficiently. People flocked from far and near to see once more that beloved face— the pallid forehead encircled by a wreath of laurel. His attached friends, his grateful pupils and admirers, with bitter tears, bade a silent and solemn farewell to the dead master. A funeral service was appointed to take place in the University church on the 7th November; at its close his coffin was to be conveyed to Berlin, and placed by Fanny's side, in the family burying-place.

On the appointed day, at four o'clock in the afternoon, the tolling of bells and the sounds of funeral music announced to the expectant throng that the procession was approaching.

The coffin was preceded by two music choirs, by the members of the Gewandhaus orchestra and the pupils of the Conservatorium, one of whom carried a silver laurel-wreath on a white satin cushion. The black pall of the coffin, embroidered in silver, was scarcely visible, so entirely was it covered with clusters of flowers, palm-branches, wreaths, and garlands. The four corners of the pall were borne by the dearest friends and art-colleagues of the deceased—Moscheles and David among others. How profoundly was every heart affected by the sounds of the glorious E minor song from the fifth book of Mendelssohn's " Songs without Words," arranged for wind instruments by Moscheles, expressly for this last solemn convoy!

Next to the coffin came the mourners, the clergy, chief civil and military authorities, the members of the University, the magistracy, the city delegates, the students, and innumerable mourners of every class. The Pauline church was hung with black, and illuminated; and while the coffin was being carried in and placed on a raised platform, a greeting floated down as from heaven itself—a prelude of Sebastian Bach. Then, accompanied by trombones and the organ, the assembled congregation sang some verses of that grandest of all choral melodies by Sebastian Bach—

O Haupt voll Blut und Wunden !

At its close, the choir commenced the choral from " St. Paul : "—

Herr, Dir will ich mich ergeben,

succeeded by a loving oration to the memory of the deceased, spoken by pastor Howard of the Reformed Church. The splendid choral that followed—

Siehe, wir preisen selig, die erduldet,

caused thousands of tears to flow.

The benediction was spoken over the beloved remains, and the final chorus from Bach's " Passionsmusik " closed the sublime solemnity.

The coffin was conveyed the same night to Berlin, accompanied by attached friends ; the greetings of mournful love and reverence the silent procession received at every station, lighting up the gloomy path like stars. In Dessau, in the midst of a vocal choir, a reverend form awaited them, with uncovered silvery hair—Friedrich Schneider, the composer of the "Weltgericht." Weeping, he received the dead young master whom in life he had so tenderly loved.

In accordance with the wishes of his family, the funeral rites in Berlin were as simple as possible. The mournful procession arrived before six o'clock in the morning. In the midst of a silent throng of notabilities in art, the decorated coffin was placed on the hearse amid the sounds of the choral, "Jesu, meine Zuversicht;" and during the transit to the church-yard, Beethoven's "Funeral March" was played. The first rays of the rising winter sun flickered on the palm branches and flowers, and— on Fanny's grave. Pastor Berduscheck, a devoted friend of the Mendelssohn family, in deep emotion, pronounced the final benediction over the corpse in few but striking words.

Wie sie so sanft ruhn!

then resounded in the silent, hallowed dawn of

day, and—all was over. Earth had received the mortal remains of one of her most beloved children.

I was at that time at Frankfort-on-the-Maine, studying in the St. Cecilia Association, with zeal and delight, "Elijah," a performance of which was to be given in the church, the soprano solos having been intrusted to me, to my pride and joy. But even during the first rehearsals, distressing reports were circulated in the town, of Mendelssohn's serious illness. It was very striking to see how the most dissimilar people were attracted to each other by this common subject of interest, stopping in the street to ask each other whether any fresh tidings had arrived from Leipzig. A heavy atmosphere seemed to oppress every heart. As for myself, I was in a state of the most feverish excitement. I wrote almost every day to my father and mother to inquire, without remembering that I could not receive a daily reply. The last rehearsal of the solos came, but I went with a heavy heart, for on the previous evening it was rumored that worse reports had arrived, and on this morning my expected letter from Leipzig had not come. The admirable Franz Messer directed at that time the St. Cecilia Association. When I entered the hall, the introduction to the duett between Elijah and the widow was about to commence. The director, in his usual lively manner, was still passing from one desk to another. I seated myself in my usual place, to await his signal, when I saw good Dr. L—— come in, as pale as death. He who always showed me such marked kindness, now only bowed gravely from a distance, and made no effort to come nearer. Several gentlemen were standing round him. The orchestra had already begun to rehearse some portions—painful uneasiness suddenly assailed me. I thought I could distinguish incessant whispering behind me; but Franz Messer gave me the signal, and I rose. While passing through the rows of the audience, I heard these words, "She must not be told of it till the rehearsal is over!" I stood still, and looked round in alarm. In an instant I was by the side of my friend, with the anxious question, " What has happened?" He took my hand with warm sympathy, and answered in a faltering voice, " Be calm, my dear child, be calm! It is only what we all expected: our Mendelssohn is dead!"

The tears of anguish shed on that memorable morning in Frankfort also formed a requiem! Messer laid down his *báton*, deeply affected; the musicians stood in silence, while in a few brief words he told them, in a voice broken with emotion, that the master whom they could never forget had gone to his long home. When, some hours later, we attempted to resume the rehearsal, our grief burst forth afresh as violently as ever. Who could sing at such a moment?

The " Elijah " was now given in commemoration of the great departed master; we all appeared in the deepest mourning, and the performance was universally admitted to have been worthy of the great composer, had he been present. How many towns offered a similar homage to the deceased!

9

The first subscription concert in Leipzig after Mendelssohn's death had a most imposing effect. The programme consisted principally of the compositions of him whose loss they were lamenting; the choruses and solos were sung by dilettanti. Compositions of the different periods of Mendelssohn's life were given in succession, in the presence of a closely thronged multitude. Among those selected were " Luther's Hymn," the enchanting Overture to the " Fair Melusine," the introduction to " St. Paul," a Motett *a cappella*, and Eichendorff's lovely " Nachtlied,"

Bright day is departed.

The sweet voice that sang this brought tears even into eyes that had long ceased to weep, and filled the heart of every hearer with the most profound emotion. Departed, too, was the bright day of *his* life; a golden harp was mute, and its strings rent asunder. Felix Mendelssohn now slept the sleep that knows no waking on this earth.

Nearly six years after the death of Mendelssohn, on the 23rd of September, 1853, the pure life of Cécile came to a close, after enduring intense sufferings, in the midst of which the patient invalid offered a bright example of pious resignation to her family.

A very dear friend of the beautiful Cécile assured me that her sorrow for the loss of him who ever dwelt in her memory was quite inconsolable, though, like every heartfelt grief, not demonstrative; but her life was gradually consumed by this secret corroding misery. She also saw one of her children die—her youngest son, Felix, followed his father. She bore her double bereavement with uncomplaining and silent resignation. She seldom spoke of her ardent longing for those who had preceded her to the grave—a longing with which, however, she reproached herself, for the sake of her beloved children, for whom she henceforth exclusively lived. She became even more and more absorbed in the remembrance of the brilliant past—those days of rare felicity. Alas! such recollections in misery are, according to the words of the poet, the most painful of all :—

> Nessun maggior dolore
> Che ricordarsi del tempo felice
> Nella miseria.

To the last moment of her life she was serene, lovely, pious, and resigned, controlling her feelings in the most heroic way, for the sake of her own fond mother, who tended her child with such touching affection. Surrounded by her loving and lamenting children, one fine autumnal evening, the pure soul of Cécile drew its latest breath in her native city —Frankfort.

Let us place a wreath on the last resting-place of the devoted wife of the deceased master—not of laurel or palm, such as decked his grave—no! a wreath in harmony with her modest retiring nature. Ludwig Berger's " Violet Song " hovers before my soul when I think of Cécile—a song that Mendelssohn so dearly loved :—

> Spirit-broken, what have I
>   To do with hopes or fears?
>   No dread have I for future years,
> No hope except to die.

Yet first I will bedeck her tomb,
  Not with the rosemary of gloom,
  But violets of sweet perfume,
And water them with tears.

My book bears for its motto a verse of Geibel's highly poetical elegy. It confirms in the most eloquent manner what I have striven to show forth—that never did a more ideal man, or more ideal artist, tread this earth than our beloved and never-to-be-forgotten Felix Mendelssohn !

APPENDICES.

No. I.

UNPUBLISHED LETTERS

OF

FELIX MENDELSSOHN-BARTHOLDY.

1.

To Hildebrandt, Düsseldorf.

Leipzig, October 31, 1835.

(While the bells are sweetly ringing for the Reformation
Feast.)

Dear Hildebrandt: . . . .
Those were indeed pleasant times when you could daily
come to the window and have a peep at me at breakfast, and thus at once give a pleasant beginning to the
day; and often have I thought of it since, when I have
been breakfasting alone, alas! and undisturbed. Moreover, I ought not just now to read through your letter
and Schirmer's if I am cordially to praise my new
abode; for, indeed, I find no compensation here for the
many happy hours we passed together, nor even anything to remind me of them. On the other hand, I
must confess that I now first discover what a vast deal,
in a musical point of view, I was cut off from at Düsseldorf, and how much unnecessary worry I endured about

many things, not to be effected by individual good-will, and how entirely I am satisfied with my public functions here. The institution of the concerts which I am engaged in, has been founded more than fifty years; all is going on in regular good order, though there are some old-fashioned traditional customs that I find almost touching, as indicative of the past, just as I might take pleasure in the pigtail or perruque of some gentleman of the olden day. The orchestra, however, are chiefly young and full of life, the playing unusually steady, and, moreover, some celebrated musicians among them. I have heard some of my Overtures given here with more *ensemble* and precision than I ever did before; and have also the satisfaction of observing that in the evenings they understand, and instantaneously execute, every suggestion or hint of my *bâton*. If you compare this with many of the rehearsals and performances we have attended together, you may well believe that I am better off here so far as music is concerned. But if even a fragment of the Academy of Painters could be transferred to Leipzig when larks are in season, life here would be far merrier. No chance of this, however, so I strive to live retired, and to work busily. If I can manage it, I intend to set out in the spring, and to take a walking tour for a couple of months; that in any event I shall then come to Düsseldorf, and some fine morning peep in to see how my friend the painter dispatches his breakfast, is an absolute certainty. A vast amount of snow and hail, and fifteen subscription concerts (five being over) still intervene between us and that time, and I trust many a letter from you, but worst of all, however, a couple of long months. Still, even now the thought cheers me, and I eagerly dwell on it. . . .

You wrote too little about yourself and your belongings; so I do beg of you, dear *Höllenbart*, to make up for this, and tell me what your family are doing—whether the Princes * still exist, or are by this time murdered, and what pictures are in your head; let me hear of the Schadows, and of you all, and also of the theater and Immermann, as it all interests me; of the Singverein and the " Rath der Alten," † and, above all, do write again soon. With cordial remembrances to you and yours,

I am yours, F. M.-B.

2.

To Friedrich Wilhelm von Schadow, Düsseldorf.

BERLIN, August 9, 1835.

DEAR HERR DIRECTOR : I cannot resist writing you a few lines from here—first of all, to inform you of the perfect health of your father, whom I saw yesterday. The first few days after our safe arrival passed away, and I repeatedly missed your father; but he came here yesterday evening, and was in as gay a mood, and as fresh as I ever saw him. He indeed complains of his

---

* The Sons of Edward IV., painted by Hildebrandt, the progress of which had been assisted by Mendelssohn's zealous criticism.

† The head society in Düsseldorf.

eyes, but he goes about the streets quite alone in the evenings, without any difficulty ; he at once recognizes
people in a room. and, as I said before, he is so cheerful
and good-humored that it is a pleasure to see him. He
complained of want of rain causing an *exhalaison* in the
town, which is an abomination to him. When I asked
him what the musical section of the Academy was doing,
he replied, " Nothing at all, my lad ! " Then he went
on to tell me about artists, and the Art Union, and a
hundred clubs—a Monday club, a chess club, and all the
others—in short, he is exactly the same as when I first
knew him long ago. I too have the happiness of finding
that people here think my father looking better than he
has done for long. The journey was anxious, tiresome
work, and doubly so because my father became very un-
well in Cassel, and was in very bad humor, to which
the slowness of the journey, the rapid changes from
heat to cold, and the intolerable dust, all contributed ;
and he was likewise harassed by his solicitude as to how
my mother would be able to bear the journey ; and so
you may imagine how I thanked God when at length
Steglitz and Schöneberg and the Gensdarmthürme came
in sight. But the first days here, too, were far from agreeable ; were obliged to decline seeing a number of visitors,
though some came and made their way in through the
garden-door, whom we were obliged, with many compliments, to bow out civilly, which of course they had
no right to take amiss ; then came the Berlin Revolution, which I feared might alarm my mother, although

she was by no means much alarmed, after all. The former home comforts for my parents are only now restored, so that we may for the first time say that the journey is over, and happily over. I shall have to remain here about eight days, and then go to Leipzig; but whether I shall have any spare time to go to Frankfort in September I cannot yet say, but would be only too glad were it so; and then, if I really got as far as Frankfort in September, I should inevitably have to come by the steamboat to visit you for a couple of days. But, as I said before, I consider this rather problematical, though I should like it so much before laying myself up in lavender or in pickle (or whatever you like to call it) for the winter in Leipzig. I write nothing whatever about Berlin. You know what has happened, and it is not cheering; no doubt, also, you already have all possible details of the great Revolution of 1835 in Berlin; it is said that 150 young ruffians were arrested, and 50 other persons. What they wanted is made clear as the day by the investigation: first, to send up rockets; not being allowed to do this, their object was to teaze and irritate the military, and they stuck pins into the horses of the dragoons, and so forth, on which everybody thrashed everybody else; all the lamps "unter den Linden" were smashed, all the benches demolished, numbers of windows broken, one of Kranzler's (the confectioner) shops sacked, while the *populus* shouted, "Come on, we'll eat ices too!" The whole of Berlin flocked to the spot, and looked on at the revolution, and next day a mass of young apprentice-boys went about singing,

Let us victory's wreath display,
No window shall be whole to-day!

When I also add that Berlin is split into two parties on the subject, the one compassionating the military and abusing the mob, the other compassionating the mob and abusing the military, and that all the world are looking forward to the approaching fishing-feast at Stralau, and making bets whether it will pass off peacefully or not—then I may say that I have portrayed the Berlin Revolution, at which I was present, with as much historical truth as ever Ranke did the Middle Ages. By way of postscript, I must inform you that it is said the windows of Princess Liegnitz have been broken, and Duke Karl's hat knocked off, and that on the Lange Brücke one young scamp said to the sentry, "Just you get out of the way, I have got this lamp to smash." If your spirit does not wax patriotic after that, I am much mistaken. I have a favor to ask of you, dear Herr Director, regarding the money I inclose. During my stay in Düsseldorf I was anxious to contribute a certain sum to the collections made weekly by the Sisters of Charity, and decided on sending them my next *honorarium;* it was, however, a long time coming, for I only received it a few days ago here. I would therefore beg of you to get the inclosed cheque cashed, and to give the money in my name to the Sisters of Charity in Düsseldorf; but it is my wish that in case the acknowledgments I have often read in the newspapers are still continued, my name may not be mentioned. Pray excuse my giving you this trouble, but I did not like to risk sending the money by post. I am told that we have acquired two beautiful new pictures in the Museum here, which I have heard highly praised—one a Murillo, the other a Zurbaran.

3.

To Friedrich Wilhelm von Schadow.

Leipzig, October 31, 1836.

Dear Herr Director: I must ask your forgiveness for my long silence; but after all, if you are angry with me, you will not read my excuses. In truth, I find it difficult even now to write to you on a subject that we discussed together so much during our dreary Dutch days, for I must either have written you everything, and thus exhausted your patience, or have said nothing but "I am betrothed to Cécile Jeanrenaud." The latter I should undoubtedly have written to you at once, had I not been strictly prohibited doing so by the family; it was to be a profound secret, and it is only since I came here that I find every one knows it, and now I feel positively ashamed to write you such stale news so late in the day. To me, indeed, it is ever quite new, and every day newer and more charming, for every day I see more unlooked-for and delightful effects from my great happiness; but still it is always mortifying to be obliged to entreat to be forgiven as humbly as I now do. I rely much on your old and tried kindness and friendship for me; otherwise indeed I should scarcely have ventured to approach you in writing, but have waited to make my excuses in person, when perhaps Cécile would have come to my aid.

I have, too, another plea to bring forward in my justification, which is that I never had so many or such fatiguing labors as since my return here, so that hitherto I have only been able to write once to my sister, and not even once to the greater portion of my most intimate friends. During the last four weeks I have conducted eight concerts, and about twenty rehearsals, and, moreover, next week there is to be a grand church performance of "Israel in Egypt" with the organ, and a concert every week up to Christmas, for which I have to make out the programme, and organize everything. I wish, too, that my own works should progress; then I have occasional pupils who occupy me daily for a couple of hours; and lastly, a number of strangers who are coming this way, and whose stay is brief, which is the most embarrassing thing of all. Last week, for example, Eduard Bendemann was here for three days, and accompanied me faithfully to my "Israel" rehearsals and others. I need not tell you how I rejoiced in being with him, nor how repeatedly we discussed the *pro* and *contra* of the Dresden Directorship, as well as others, though without coming to any fixed result. On the day of his departure, Hauptmann, from Cassel, a kind musical friend of mine, suddenly appeared, and stayed two days; then my cousin from Aix passed through with his whole family ; and the same day arrived the young Englishman Bennett, who intends to remain here the whole winter; and finally, yesterday, came Berger, my first pianoforte teacher, and called on me; and thus it goes on day by day. And yet I would give my life to be at the Fahr-thor at Frankfort, and to let concerts alone, and not be obliged to wait till Christmas, when I intend certainly to be in Frankfort, though only for ten days, for on the 1st of January I must be here again, working away at music till Easter, which is so very obliging to me as to fall very early next year, so there is a good time coming for me. But when the last concert is over, I intend, God willing, to get into a carriage at once, and set off. Whether I shall be here next winter, or elsewhere, is still quite uncertain.

I should like to have seen the Exhibition in Berlin (and still more my own family); but that, too, must be deferred, as I cannot find the time requisite for even so short an absence. It is very evident that under such circumstances I cannot properly cultivate the plastic arts according to the principles I acquired at the Hague, and my men and women have exactly the same disloca-ted arms and legs that they had before you took the trouble to set their limbs again.

May I beg of you to give many kind and cordial wishes from me to your good wife? I know that she will sincerely sympathize with my joy, and I hope that she is satisfied with me for having so well profited by

9*

her advice. My happiness is due more to my good fortune than to my good sense—at least, there are often times when I cannot at all understand how I have attained such felicity; meanwhile, that it is mine in reality I can no longer doubt, and every fresh letter thence confirms this anew. As I have hitherto acted so entirely in accordance with the counsels of the Frau Directorin, I think I may venture to ask her a little favor, which is to let me have here for a few days that sketch of mine of Amalfi, in Indian ink, now in her album; you know, dear Herr Director, that I was formerly very anxious to copy it for my bride (it must be this particular view, because a legend is attached to it), but could not get it at the time, the book being locked up. You will therefore confer a great pleasure on me if you will send me the drawing, and allow me to keep it to copy till Christmas, when I will return it without fail, and with many thanks. I scarcely dare to hope for a few lines in return, dear Herr Director, for I know your time scarcely admits of it, and I also dread being soundly scolded, but I must once more entreat you not to withdraw your friendship from me, and not to be angry with me, and to believe that always, even in the most momentous period of my life, I am, and ever shall be, your devoted

FELIX MENDELSSOHN.

4.

To Herr Schloss, Cologne.

THE HAGUE, August 7, 1836.

SIR: In compliance with the wish expressed in your esteemed letter, which I did not receive till yesterday here, I now give you in writing my opinion of the musical talent of your daughter, and shall rejoice if I can thus in any degree contribute to her welfare and her future career. I am, with esteem, your obedient

FELIX MENDELSSOHN-BARTHOLDY

Testimonial.

THE HAGUE, August 7, 1836.

M'lle Sophie Schloss, whom I had the opportunity of hearing some months ago in Düsseldorf, possesses a remarkably fine, powerful, melodious, mezzo-soprano voice, which in purity and clearness of tone leaves little to be desired. Not having hitherto had any chance of properly cultivating this fine organ, it is highly desirable that she should have an opportunity of perfecting herself in the technical part of singing, both in execution, and in the mode of rendering and pronouncing. As her voice also seems flexible and sympathetic, and she is exceedingly musical, I am convinced that with a good model and proper instruction she will become a most admirable singer. She sings well and correctly at sight, which is another decisive proof of her musical capacities, a good ear being combined with a beautiful organ.

FELIX MENDELSSOHN-BARTHOLDY.

5.

To Herr Schloss.

LEIPZIG, January 31, 1839.

DEAR SIR: I was happy to find in your esteemed letter tidings of the progress and improvement of your daughter. The deficiency in distinguished vocal talent in Germany is at this moment so great, that the appearance of any one conspicuous in this department will be joyfully welcomed on all sides. If your daughter is disposed to settle here, and the opinion of her merits expressed in your letter be correct, and formed from intimate knowledge, I do not in that case doubt that the directors of our concerts will offer her an advantageous engagement from next autumn. The place of a concert singer chances to be vacant here at present, and if your daughter has decided on this profession, she could scarcely, in the whole of Germany, meet with a more lucrative or agreeable engagement. It would be a source of sincere pleasure to me to procure it for her; but before I can do so, or recommend her, it is absolutely indispensable that I should hear her again myself, and no doubt there will soon be an opportunity for this. I am going to the Rhine in April, and beg you will write me a line to say whether I may expect to meet your daughter then at Cologne. Should that be the case, I shall lose no time in at once paying her a visit, when I can also confer with you better on every point in person than by writing I would willingly give you a letter of introduction to Herr Guhr, but I have too slight a personal acquaintance with him to do so. I am, Sir, with esteem, your obedient

FELIX MENDELSSOHN-BARTHOLDY.

6.

To Herr Schloss.

FRANKFORT-ON-THE-MAINE, June 11, 1839.

DEAR SIR: I have just received the answer to my letter from the Directors of the Leipzig concerts concerning your daughter, and I hasten to communicate it to you. From the praise I bestowed on your daughter's talent, and could not fail to bestow in accordance with truth and a good conscience, the Directors write that they have unanimously resolved to offer your daughter an engagement for the approaching winter's concerts, hoping that she may be disposed to conclude a longer and more important one for the following years. They offer her a salary of 400 dollars, and 60 dollars for traveling expenses, and further, their aid and support in the prosecution of her vocal studies, during or after the first season, in Dresden, under the guidance of Cicimara, or some other experienced teacher of singing, and they hope that these proposals may prove acceptable. There are twenty concerts in the course of the season, which succeed each other almost every week, and continue from the first Sunday after Michaelmas till the week before Easter. Your daughter would have to sing in some an aria and a cavatina, in others an aria and a *morceau d'ensemble*, or possibly only an *ensemb'e* piece; the more arias and cavatinas, therefore, that she studies correctly and carefully, the better.

So much for the commission of the Concert Direction. I hope it may be satisfactory to you, and am convinced that if your daughter accepts the offer, she will be contented with her residence at Leipzig; anything I can do to contribute to this shall be gladly done; and in every respect the winter here is not devoid of interest, as most of the distinguished artists visit Leipzig in order to be heard there, so that in few places is there a better opportunity to cultivate and to develop ability and taste. It would give me great pleasure to know that the Concert Institute possessed so fine a talent, and I am certain that all the Directors will agree with me in this respect. On the other hand, I trust that your daughter, more especially if she makes a longer stay in the Institute, will take pleasure in it, and like being there.

I beg you will send me your answer here as soon as possible, to the care of Herr Souchay, and I am, with esteem, yours,

Felix Mendelssohn-Bartholdy.

7.

To Sophie Schloss, Leipzig.

Leipzig, September 3), 1839.

My Dear Young Lady: I thought I had already mentioned to you in Frankfort that the Concert Directors here make it a condition with the singers they engage, that they are not to sing in any public concerts, except in the subscription ones, so long as their engagement lasts. Whether I did not express myself distinctly, or whether you did not hear me, I cannot say, but at all events it is a stipulation which has hitherto always been enforced on others, and of course will be so in your case also. Exceptions might indeed be made *with the consent of the Directors*, and it would be particularly agreeable to me that such should be the case in Herr Panofka's concert in particular; I will therefore make the necessary application myself to the Directors, and endeavor to gain their consent. In the conference, however, from which I have just returned, a directly contrary opinion was distinctly given, so I beg you on no account to pledge yourself either to Herr Panofka, or to any one else, till I can inform you more minutely of what may occur in the course of to-morrow. I am yours with high esteem,

FELIX MENDELSSOHN-BARTHOLDY.

8.

To Sophie Schloss, Cologne.

LEIPZIG, July 23, 1841.

MY DEAR YOUNG LADY: Difficult as it is to give really good and serviceable advice on so important an affair as the one to which you allude, still I do not hesitate to give you my honest opinion on the point, were it only in order to prove to you the interest I have always taken, and always shall take, in all that concerns yourself and your talent. As you are resolved to go on the stage, the offer of an engagement from Weimar seems to be highly satisfactory, and were I in your place I should certainly endeavor to secure it at once. You will there have an opportunity of spending the most trying time for a theatrical artist—I mean the first years on the stage—in a good school, under the guidance of experienced artists, and appear before a cultivated, and yet not too exac'ing, public. When these are once over, and happily over everything is gained; but on that very account it is most important to pass those first years in a well-managed theater, where you have plenty of work and good stage practice. All this is the case in Weimar; but, if I am not mistaken, the salaries are very small. In my opinion, therefore, during the first two years, or the first year at all events, you ought to be as moderate as possible in your demands; only ask just enough to be able to live on your salary, as many young singers during the first years sing without any payment, merely in order to become familiar with stage routine, and make up the money they thus lose by subsequent good engagements, which, when you have acquired experience, you are certain to get. Were I in your position, I would ask about 600 dollars, though I do not doubt that you excel many singers who receive more than double that sum; but I am anxious you should not, by exorbitant demands, deter the Directors from any further negotiations, and thus break off the whole affair, which I should consider a great misfortune for you at this moment. Pray endeavor, then, to come to terms with the theater at Weimar, taking advantage of this early and most important period for zealous studies and persevering exertions, and may Heaven guide you to peace and happiness on the path you are now entering, and to the harmonious development of your talents. I am, with sincere esteem, yours,

FELIX MENDELSSOHN-BARTHOLDY.

9.

To Sophie Schloss, Leipzig.

LEIPZIG, December 29, 1842.

MY DEAR YOUNG LADY: I beg you will send me the Duett we were speaking of from "Lucia;" and as you seem disposed to remain here for the next concert, I in that case request you to study and to prepare for it the Aria with pianoforte by Mozart, the part of "Fidalma" in the Trio of the "Matrimonio Segreto," "Io faccio un inchino," and the Septett in "Don Juan" that I recently sent you. Should you not have the first or second piece, I will procure them for you. With sincere esteem, yours,

FELIX MENDELSSOHN-BARTHOLDY.

10.

To Sophie Schloss.

LEIPZIG, November 2, 1846.

MY DEAR YOUNG LADY: As a rehearsal in the theater here renders it impossible to arrange another concert rehearsal on Thursday, I would earnestly request you—

1. To be in the Gewandhaus as early as possible on Wednesday morning.

2. Most *carefully* previously to study the Finale in "Euryanthe," that you may be *quite sure* of the time, notes, etc. It is a *difficult* piece, and on Tuesday we are to have a rehearsal for all those engaged in it. If you are perfectly sure of your part, it will go well, but without that it cannot possibly do so; I would therefore once more urgently entreat you to devote some time to the study of this piece. We had better reserve Mozart's Aria for one of our future concerts, so that you will only have to co-operate in the Finale from "Euryanthe" next Thursday. I shall therefore the more confidently expect the fulfillment of the wish I have expressed above. With sincere esteem, yours,

FELIX MENDELSSOHN-BARTHOLDY.

11.

To Sophie Schloss.

LEIPZIG, March 26, 1847.

DEAR YOUNG LADY: I could not manage to bring together this evening the eight requisite singers, and therefore beg you to reserve your kind assistance for one evening next week. I trust you will comply with my wish, and on that occasion sing the " Angel " as well as the detestable " Queen," both of which lie within the compass of your voice, but the former I think *far the best.* Your devoted

FELIX MENDELSSOHN-BARTHOLDY.

12.

To Sophie Schloss.

DEAR YOUNG LADY: Oh heavens! We shall go on misunderstanding each other from Thursday to Monday.

Now, which are the two Arias that you wish to sing on Thursday?—or rather, what is the particular one you wish to sing *in addition* to that of Meyerbeer, the text of which you have just sent me? Is it the one from "Oberon?" or if that does not quite suit you, then choose one of the Italian airs you sang last year. To me it is quite the same. But I do beg you will let me have your decision by the bearer. Your devoted

FELIX MENDELSSOHN-BARTHOLDY.

LETTERS TO MR. BARTHOLOMEW, Etc.

1.

To Mr. Alfred Novello.

[Written in English.]

Leipzig, November 18, 1837.

My Dear Sir : It is now a fortnight since your sister first appeared here in public. and directly after it I wanted to write to you, and give you a full account of it, and only to-day I have leisure enough to do it. Excuse it ; but although it is late, and I may think that you heard already from other sides of all the details of her great success here, I cannot help writing you also on the subject ; and before all *I* should "triumph," be-cause you know that you were my enemy,* and that my opinion prevailed only with great difficulty, and that it comes now out how well I knew my countrymen, how well they appreciate what is really good and beautiful, and what a service to all the lovers of music has been done by your sisters, coming over to this country. I do not know whether she thinks the same of my opinion now ; I am sometimes afraid she must find the place so

---

* In allusion to Mr. A. Novello's desire that his sister should pro-ceed direct to Italy, and not visit Germany.

very small and dull, and miss her splendid Philharmonic band, and all those Marchionesses, and Duchesses, and Lady Patronesses, who look so beautifully aristocratically in your concert-rooms, and of whom we have a great want. But if being really and heartily liked and loved by a public, and being looked on as a most distinguished and eminent talent, must also convey a feeling of pleasure to those that are the object of it, I am sure that your sister cannot repent her resolution of accepting the invitation to this place, and must be glad to think of the delight she gave, and the many friends she made in so short time, and in a foreign country. Indeed, I never heard such an unanimous expression of delight as after her first recitative, and it was a pleasure to see people at once agreeing, and the difference of opinion (which must always prevail) consisting only in the more or less praise to be bestowed on her. It was capital that not one hand's applause received her when she first appeared to sing "Non più di fiori," because the triumph after the recitative was the greater; the room rung of applause, and after it there was such a noise of conversations, people expressing their delight to each other, that not a note of the whole ritornello could be heard; then silence was again restored; and after the air, which she really sang better and with more expression than I ever heard from her, my good Leipzig public became like mad, and made a most tremendous noise. Since that moment she was the declared favorite of them; they are equally delighted with her clear and youthful voice, and with the purity and good taste with which she sings everything. The polacca of the "Puritani" was encored, which is a rare thing in our concerts here; and I am quite sure the longer she stays, and the more she is heard, the more she will become a favorite, because she possesses just those two qualities of which the public is particularly fond here—purity of intonation and a thoroughbred musical feeling. I must also add, that I never heard her to greater advantage than at these two concerts, and that I liked her singing infinitely better than ever I did before; whether it might be that the smaller room suits her better, or perhaps the foreign air, or whether it is that I am partial to everything in this country (which is also not unlikely), but I really think her much superior to what I have heard her before. And therefore I am once more glad that I conquered you, my enemy.

They are now in correspondence with the Court of Dessau and with Berlin, whereto they intend to go during the intervals of the concerts here; I hope, however, that their stay will be prolonged as much as possible. We had Vieuxtemps here, who delighted the public; we also expect Blagrove in the beginning of January. Charles Kemble with his daughter Adelaide passed also by this place, but she did not sing in public, only at a party at my house. Has Mr. Coventry received my letter, and the one for Bennett I sent him? And have you received the parcel with my Concerto, which Breitkopf & Härtel promised to send in great haste? Do you see Mr. Klingemann sometimes? And how is music going on in England? Or had you no time to think now of anything else than the Guildhall puddings and pies, and the 200 pine-apples which the Queen ate there, as a French paper has it? If you see Mr. Attwood, will you tell him my best compliments and wishes, and that a very great cause of regret to me is my not having been able to meet him at my last stay in England. And now the paper is over, and consequently the letter also. Excuse its style, which is probably very German. My kindest regard to Mr. and Mrs. Clarke, and my best thanks for his kind letter and the papers he sent me by Miss Novello. And now good-bye, and be as well and happy as I always wish you to be. Very truly yours,

FELIX MENDELSSOHN-BARTHOLDY. ,

About 1840 Mr. Bartholomew was told by Mr. Buxton (then the sole proprietor of the eminent house known as Ewer & Co.) that Mendelssohn had never been able to meet with a libretto which pleased him, either in Germany or England, and advised Mr. Bartholomew to make the attempt. Mr. Bartholomew wrote one of a fairy-like character, entitled "A Christmas Night's Dream." Although it did not wholly satisfy the gifted composer, it led to a lasting friendship, and caused Mendelssohn to place everything in Mr. Bartholomew's hands for English versions until the time of his lamented death, as the following letters will prove.—*Note by Mrs. Bartholomew.*

2.

To Mr. Bartholomew.

[Written in English.]

BERLIN, October 4, 1841.

SIR: You have given me a very great treat by sending me the libretto of your "Christmas Night's Dream," in which I found so many and so striking poetical beauties that I really cannot sufficiently express to you my admiration and my sincere gratitude for it. The only objection I have to it is one which Mr. Klingemann most likely had in view when he wrote the words to which you allude in your letter, but which he does not seem to have expressed, as I feel it. He calls it monotony, and finds fault with the subject itself—with the fairies and all their kindred. I cannot share this opinion; but I think that the elements, *as you conceive them,* could have been treated in a more dramatic way. In the course of the first act, Earth is spoken of as a contrast to the fairy region; Amor is several times warned of the cares of mortals, of their misery, their wants, etc.; yet these are not brought forward in the subsequent action, for the separation which he must endure in the beginning of the third act is not what we imagine alone when we hear those words in the first act, and besides, we see immediately that the separation is only a whim of Oberon, which has no necessity in itself, and comes too late in the course of the drama to excite real fear or compassion.

Also, the fairies I think would come out much better

if a real earthly life would have been opposed to their fanciful one. The beautiful verses themselves, and the imaginative songs they sing, seem to demand such a contrast, and can only produce the impression which they ought when combined with those earthly elements. Bottom and his company are certainly essential to the fanciful impression produced by the " Midsummer Night's Dream," and they are not only the first but the second contrast to the fairies, Theseus and the lovers forming the first. Something like this is what I want in your libretto, and the only thing I want in it. Without such a contrast I doubt that it could form a truly effective Opera, at least I do not think myself equal to it.

But the delightful details in which it abounds have so thoroughly fascinated me, that I hope and trust I shall one day have the good luck of writing my music to your beautiful words. The duet of Puck and Amor, when the first asks him all sorts of questions, the delightful opening scene of the second act with the bird's language, the fairies' song with the lovers' duet after it, Eudora's waking afterward, are true gems which it is impossible to read without emotion, without thinking of music, and without thanking the poet who invented them. I do not know whether you will think of altering this libretto, for it would not only be a very difficult task, but the question also is whether my impression is not only a personal one, and whether others would not judge it in quite different a way. At all events, let me hope, as I said before, that I may once be happy enough to find a

10

libretto which unites the dramatic development which I have in my idea to so extraordinary poetical beauties, so musical verses, and such a fine and noble feeling as that which pervades your whole work, and accept my best and sincerest thanks for it. Let me consider our acquaintance as begun under the auspices of your poetry, and let me hope that it may soon continue and last long. My best thanks also for the beautiful lyrics,* which I will try to set to music, as soon as I shall have a moment's leisure by myself; and believe me to be, with the greatest respect, your obedient servant,

FELIX MENDELSSOHN-BARTHOLDY.

3.

To Mr. Bartholomew.

[Written in English.]

JULY, 1842.

MY DEAR SIR: It is with true regret, and only from the deep conviction that sincerity is in all cases the best and most necessary thing, and that particularly so in an undertaking like that which we have been talking over in our last conversation, that I must write you that my views of a subject for an Opera are not entirely agreeing with the one you have selected for your recent work, and that I could, accordingly, not set it to music, although I had the most anxious desire of doing so.

It is, as you thought yourself, according to my opinion, more fit for a Melodrama than an Opera; at least, I could

---

* A poem on Music, inclosed by Mr. Bartholomew.

not reconcile it to the ideas which I have of the last, and do not think it fits the operatic form as it would another, perhaps.

But I wish I could express to you how deeply I regret this, and how truly indebted I feel, and shall always feel, for the very great kindness you have shown me in this, and indeed in every instance since the beginning of our acquaintance. Have my best, my most heartfelt thanks, for it; and allow me to repeat the expression of my admiration of your translation of "Jessonda" (which I beg to return herewith), which has given me the greatest pleasure while I perused it, and which has once more given me the greatest respect for your poetical and lyrical powers, and for the most extraordinary skill with which you have succeeded in this very difficult (and to so many others, impossible) task.*

And now, farewell! To-morrow, early, I must leave this country, and hope we shall soon meet again, and you will always continue the same kind and indulgent friend I have found you.

Always and very faithfully yours,
Felix Mendelssohn-Bartholdy.

4.

To Mr. Bartholomew.

[Written in English.]

Leipzig, January 3, 1843.

My Dear Mr. Bartholomew: Have my best thanks

---

* The English version being adapted without any of the notation being altered; a very unusual thing in a work of this extent.

for the great pleasure which your translation of the "Antigone" choruses has afforded me.* Indeed I do not know how to express sufficiently the admiration for the wonderful task you have performed, and the gratitude I feel for the most valuable assistance which you have given to the cause of my music—or rather, the cause of the King of Prussia, whose idea it was—or rather the cause of old Sophocles, whose idea the whole was. Accept a thousand most heartfelt thanks for all you have done. I am sorry I have not received the whole of the music, with your translation to it, and hope the rest is at present on its way to Leipzig. Should it not, and should this arrive in time, pray ask Mr. Buxton to let me see the rest also, before it is published. In those proofs I have seen, I took the liberty of pointing out a few passages where I would have wished an alteration in the words. I marked those passages thus (x?); it is particularly the case where there are syllables to the notes which I had slurred, and where I should wish them to remain slurred, if possible. You will excuse this, and the few questions which I wrote on the margin.

Do you call the earth *Tella* in English, and the family of the "Edonen" also with our German termination?

---

* "Antigone" was first performed at Covent Garden Theater in January, 1845, and had a run of twenty-seven consecutive nights. The abridged version, written by command of Her Majesty, was given at Buckingham Palace and Windsor Castle on various occasions, the readings being assigned to Mr. C. Kemble and Mr. Bartholomew, or Mr. Bartley and Mr. Bartholomew.—*Note by Mrs. Bartholomew.*

I sent the metronomes to Mr. Buxton, but could not get the business of the stage, which I have written at greater length in my letter to Mr. Buxton. And now once more have my sincerest thanks; present my compliments to the Misses Mounsey, whose organ-playing I always recollect with so much pleasure, and believe me always to remain, yours very truly,

FELIX MENDELSSOHN-BARTHOLDY.

5.

To Mr. Bartholomew.

[Written in English.]

LEIPZIG, June 12, 1843.

MY DEAR SIR: Pray do not be angry at receiving my very late reply to your two very kind letters. I found the second after a stay at Berlin, where I had a great deal to do (musical and otherwise), and since my return this is the first day that I am at liberty; for not only had I a great many compositions going on in my head and on my desk, but the life in my house was so busy, and so many foreign friends came and went, that I felt almost giddy every evening, when I thought of the day. Excuse me, then! I am afraid my answer about the " Antigone " choruses will be always the same. If they are to be performed at a concert, I prefer a selection of three or four ; a few which, to select, I must submit to others ; at any rate, the one in D ought to be placed as the last, and the one in E minor ought not to be left out, if possible. And now another pardon I have to ask ! I cannot as yet agree to the version of the Lied in the " Festgesang." Pray do not be very angry with me! I even liked your first version better than the one you last sent. This last is a mixture of both, which I do not think effective; and indeed your introduction of Guttenberg and of the art of printing in English verse, makes me aware that the difficulty is greater than I thought at first. I am almost sure now that the Guttenberg and the graphic pen, and all that, is not the thing, and that nothing of the kind should be mentioned in the poem.

But what then? you will say. I answer with the French proverb, " criticizing is easy, but art is difficult." I do not know, but I neither wish the creation of man nor the creation of typography, and yet I wish for something national, popular, and lofty at the same time. I am sure you would wish I was in the Pepper Country (as we say in Germany).

And now, once more, many hearty thanks for the poem you sent about the " Midsummer Night's Dream " and my overture to it. I do not know whether I am allowed to praise your poem very much, for it praises my music by far too much ; but, at any rate, I am allowed to thank you from my heart for your continued benevolence and kindness and friendship, and to assure you that I shall always be, yours very very truly,

FELIX MENDELSSOHN-BARTHOLDY.

6.

To Mr. Bartholomew.

[Written in English.]

LEIPZIG, July 17, 1813.

MY DEAR SIR: Many thanks for your kindness, for your last letter, for the new translation, for everything! Of course I like your verses very much, but you must not be angry if I still am as stubborn as an old post. The idea of a jubilate, of " Praise the Lord," etc., to that song of mine, has something in itself which hurts me. This is not the strain in which I would sing a jubilate, a " Praise the Lord." While I read it just now again and again, an idea struck me: could you not adhere to the first word of the German verses, and make this eternal No. 2, instead of a jubilate, a song in honor to *your* country, to your " Vaterland." *That* is the sense of my music; if it is "Praise the Land " instead of the " Lord," then my music is right; or perhaps " Happy Land," or " Happy thou," or, etc. Really, the more I think of it, the more I think it could and should be done so! The first two stanzas in favor of your English " Vaterland," and the third where the G minor commences, speaking of darkness, of bad times which may surround that country's horizon for a little while, but which must soon vanish before the sun, and ending with that same " Happy Land," or happy anything, as the others. This national feeling is at least the only thing which, to my idea, the music can truly express; sacred it will never be, and the more sacred the words are, the less my notes will seem so. If you approve of this idea, it would involve indeed a general alteration, the whole would become much more of a hymn to God, the Creator of England, than to Him the Creator of the world—but so much the better.

Mr. Buxton, who visits Germany in August, as I understand, shall bring you the brass score as a small atonement for this endless trouble. For God's sake do not let my old sin of " Camacho's Wedding " be stirred up again! I was fifteen years old when I wrote it, and still think it good enough for that age, but certainly not for that venerable one which I have attained now, and in which I would be able to do something better. So pray keep it *entre nous*, and always believe me yours very excessively, truly, and thankfully,

FELIX MENDELSSOHN-BARTHOLDY.

7.

To Mr. Bartholomew.

[Written in English.]

LEIPZIG, July 31, 1843.

MY DEAR SIR: Many thanks for yesterday's letter with the translation of the six songs. I like it very much, and have only a few trifling objections to make—none to any of them as a whole, but only to some details. Your despair about Eichendorff's poetry has made me laugh very much; it is a very odd thing, and meant to be so, and would sound still more wild if translated literally. I think your version a very good one, and as a whole it corresponds with the German meaning perfectly, although I miss some details—"O Lieb, O liebe," etc. (which, by-the-by, is *not* addressed to a lady), for which I am not sorry at all, as it sings, and is much easier understood, and is indeed much more the thing than a more literal translation would be. My objections (for you see I am the eternal objector) are :—

1. In No. 2, the last two stanzas, and more particularly the last, and more particularly the last two lines, and most particularly the Corydon in them. Pray don't let us have Corydon, or any such name, in it! I could never reconcile it to my feelings, if Corydon, or Phyllis, or Damon came in at the end. I would even wish that neither he nor she was mentioned, and that it was a something of love which the tenor and bass could say as well as the soprano and alto. So it is in the German, although it does not seem so, and although it is rather a difficult passage, of which a literal translation would not do at all.

There are some more objections I have in that song. " Now Zephyr rushes, onward he goes; " there I should prefer something more literal, because it is one of the greatest beauties of the poem. The " mätchtiger," " more powerful," ought to be expressed if possible as well as the " doch er verlieret," " but it vanishes :" this contrast is so beautifully expressive of spring-time. Then I would wish in the beginning of the last but one stanza to have the German expression, " Zum Busen kehrt er zurück," "It returns to the bosom"—at least, the *returning*, because it is this word that gave me the idea of coming back to the first subject, and it does therefore well with the music.   And then it is so fine in the poetry to follow the Zephyr (or what wind it may be) on its way; beginning first "more powerfully," "vanishing" then directly in the bushes, and returning at last to the bosom, or the feeling of the poet! but, before all, pray kill Corydon, because I detest him amazingly.

In No. 4 could you adhere still closer to the German, " Was neues hat sie nicht gelernt," "she has not learnt a novel lay" (She sings the old that nature taught her)? I think it the "point" of the poem.   And last of all, the last line of all, "Gay as the feathers that dance in their crests," is not just what I could wish for my music's sake.   If you could find there another simile, something less *chevaleresque* and more poetical in itself, some simile taken from the wind, or the spring, or the bushes, or anything of the kind, but not of the feathers.

Now pray forgive my fastidiousness, and have my best thanks for the difficult task you have again so masterly done.

The altered notes, as you propose them, will suit me completely.

Believe me, my dear Sir, with many true thanks, always yours,

FELIX MENDELSSOHN-BARTHOLDY.

Pray tell Mr. Buxton that I think very much of a new book of "Lieder ohne Worte," and that I intend publishing one still in the course of this year, which I will send immediately, when ready. And tell him also, pray, that I will not send the music of the "erste Walpurgisnacht" before I have talked it over with him, because I am rather doubtful whether the style of the thing (poem as well as music) would do for the English, and because the opportunity of discussing this with him, and seeing him here, is now so close at hand. I expect him, then, toward the end of August. Add my best compliments to the long message. And pray forward the inclosed to my friend Klingemann, and excuse all this trouble!

Some sacred concerts being held in London under the direction of Miss Mounsey (now Mrs. Mounsey Bartholomew), Mr. Bartholomew wrote to request Dr. Mendelssohn would compose something for one of these performances, taking the words from Scripture, or from either of the three accompanying sets of verses. Mendelssohn selected one of those, "Hear my prayer," and this composition for a soprano and chorus (now held in such high esteem in this country) was transmitted with the following gratifying letter to Mr. Bartholomew.—*Note by Mrs. Bartholomew.*

8.

To Mr. Bartholomew.

[Written in English.]

BERLIN, January 31, 1844.

MY DEAR SIR: I send you the sacred solo * which

---

* "Hear my Prayer!"

you wanted me to write for your concerts at Crosby
Hall, and beg you will keep the manuscript as a token
of my sincere gratitude and respect.

You have been so often so kind to me, that I am almost
ashamed of the trifle I offer in return; however, I have
nothing better, and so you must " take the will for the
deed."

It is a little after the time you fixed me for sending the
music, but I hope, as you receive it early in February,
that it will yet be in time for the last concert at least.

I have only to observe that the bass of the organ accompaniment is always meant to be played either with the
pedals, or with the lower octave in the left hand, which
I never wrote in it. *

Be as healthy and as happy as I always wish you to
be; and remember kindly, yours very truly,

FELIX MENDELSSOHN-BARTHOLDY.

9.

To Mr. Bartholomew.

[Written in English.]

LEIPZIG, March 21, 1846.

MY DEAR SIR: I owe to you many many thanks for
two very kind letters. And not for the letters only.
Still more for the copy of your English version of
" Antigone " which you sent with the first, and which I

---

* The following year Mendelssohn sent various little alterations
to this work; these and the original manuscript are now in the
possession of Mrs. Bartholomew.—*Note by Mrs. Bartholomew.*

admire so much and value so highly! And for the account of the performance of it at the Palace which your second letter conveyed to me! For this, and for all the trouble you have taken with it, and for the good you have done to it, I wish I could thank you sufficiently and express my gratitude as I feel it.

But to-day I have not only to thank you for past kindnesses, but I intend to ask you for new proofs of it, and I will ask a new favor, almost before I have been able to thank you for the former ones. Your Queen sent for a copy of my score to the " Athalia " of Racine, which I dispatched to London yesterday; and next week I hope to send a copy of the choruses of " Œdipus " to Mr. Anderson, who wanted to have them for the Prince. I wrote already to Mr. Anderson to say that I wished *you* to undertake the translation of these last choruses; but, as the score of the " Athalia " was ordered through Lord Westmoreland, I could not mention it to *him*. But I wish you would do them both, if your leisure does allow you to do so; and this is the request which I have to make to you now, and by the complying with which you would confer a new and very great obligation on me.

Believe me, my dear Sir, always and very sincerely and gratefully yours,

FELIX MENDELSSOHN-BARTHOLDY.

10.

*To Baroness Dorothea Ertmann.**

LEIPZIG, April 12, 1846.

DEAR AND HIGHLY ESTEEMED BARONESS : I have not
written to you since our never-to-be-forgotten days in
Milan, and probably you scarcely know how deeply my
heart is penetrated with profound and unchanging gratitude toward you. Few days have passed since then
without my thinking long and often of your kindness
and friendship, and thanking you anew ; and I have

---

* Dorothea Freifran von Ertmann was a native of Offenbach,
daughter of a wealthy merchant. She commenced her musical
studies early in life. Though her talents were great, she had not
much perseverance, so she was literally often tied to the music-stool
by her mother. At the age of eighteen she became the wife of an
Austrian captain, Baron von Ertmann, who subsequently died in
Milan as a field-marshal. The Baroness made the acquaintance of
Beethoven in Vienna by a singular chance. She saw in Tobias
Haslinger's musical catalogue the names of some recently published
sonatas of Beethoven, played them at sight in an adjoining room,
and was quite enchanted with their genial flow. When she had
fin'shed playing, a shy and awkward young man came into the room
and presented himself to her as the composer. From that time
Beethoven was in the habit of dai'y frequenting the house of the
Baroness, and teaching her his sonatas. In his intercourse with
her he was as severe and gruff, as sens'tive and eccentric as ever,
but met with the utmost forbearance and patience on the part of
the Baroness. Although, in spite of this, he sometimes absented
himself for weeks in a sulky humor, still he always at length came
back ; and when the Baroness lost the last of her children,
Beethoven's sorrow was great. In the course of a few weeks he
expressed his sympathy by music, and while she was seated beside
him at the piano, he extemporized in the most enchanting tones.
When he closed his fantasia, tears prevented her speaking, and he
left the room. His sonata in A major, Op. 101, is dedicated to the
Baroness. She had all his sonatas, with Beethoven's own annota-
tions.

been also much impressed by all that is good and praise-
worthy in your life, which has come to my knowledge
since we met, though, living so far away, I could not
communicate my feelings to you. After the lapse of so
many long years, an opportunity has just occurred to
write to you which I cannot allow to escape, knowing
that I can afford you pleasure. My friend Jenny Lind
is going to Vienna, and I am anxious that you should
become acquainted; for a more noble, estimable, or true
and thorough artist I never in my life met, and I know
well that I cannot cause you greater joy than by intro-
ducing her to you. Were she to sing to you a little song
or a grand aria, it would be quite unnecessary for me to
say anything on the subject; so, as you are sure to hear
her, I need add no more. I have only one more request
to make, which is, that you will sometimes bestow a
friendly thought on me. The hours I once passed in
your house were so very delightful! If you wish to
hear any further details of my career, M'lle Lind can
relate them more minutely, as I have seen her so frequently that she knows every particular with regard to
myself and my family. I trust you will rely on the
unchangeable devotion and heartfelt gratitude with
which I shall through life ever remain your devoted,

FELIX MENDELSSOHN-BARTHOLDY.

11.

To Mr. Bartholomew.

[Written in English.]   LEIPZIG, May 11, 1846.

MY DEAR SIR: Many thanks for your kind letter of

the 4th, to which I hasten to reply, and to tell you that the Oratorio for the Birmingham Festival is *not* the "Athalia" (nor the "Œdipus," of course), but a much greater, and (to me) more important work than both together;* that it is not quite yet finished, but that I write continually, to finish it in time; and that I intend sending over the first part (the longest of the two it will have) in the course of the next ten or twelve days. I asked Mr. Moore from Birmingham to have it translated by you, and I have no doubt he will communicate with you about it, as soon as he gets my letter, which I wrote four or five days ago; and I beg you will be good enough, if you can undertake it, to try to find some leisure time toward the end of this month, that the choral parts with English words, may be as soon as possible in the hands of the chorus-singers. And pray give it your best English words, for till now I feel so much more interest in this work than for my others, and I only wish it may last so with me. Always very truly yours,

FELIX MENDELSSOHN-BARTHOLDY.

12.

To Mr. Bartholomew.

[Written in English.]

LEIPZIG, July 28, 1846.

MY DEAR SIR: Here are the metronomes, which I beg you will give the director of the choruses; but tell him

---

* The Oratorio in course of composition proved to be the "Elijah." —*Note by Mrs. Bartholomew.*

that I cannot promise they will be *exactly* the same, but *nearly* so, I think.

Many thanks for your last letter, with the remarks about the song.* I do not recollect having heard the Scotch ballad to which you allude,† and certainly did not think of it, and did not *choose* to imitate it; but as mine is a song to which I always had an objection (of another kind), and as the ballad seems much known, and the likeness very striking, and before all, as you wish it, I shall leave it out altogether (I think), and have altered the two last bars of the preceding recit., so that the chorus in F may follow it immediately. Perhaps I shall bring another song in its stead, but I doubt it, and even believe it to be an improvement if it is left out.

You receive here No. 36, 38 and 39. The only piece which is now not in your hands is No. 37, a song of Elijah. And this (and perhaps one song to be introduced in the first part) I shall either send or bring myself, for they will require only few words, and it will be plenty of time to copy the vocal parts, and the instrumental ones I bring over with me. I hope to be in London on the 17th, and beg you will let us have a grand meeting on the 18th, to settle all the questions and the copies of the solo parts.

Always yours very truly,
FELIX MENDELSSOHN-BARTHOLDY.

---

* 'Oh! rest in the Lord!" † "Auld Robin Gray."

10*

13.

To R. Bowley, Esq.

[Written in English.]

[Received Sept. 7, 1846.]

Sir: I am very sorry to be obliged to inform you, that in consequence of a letter from Birmingham, which I received this morning, I must give up the pleasure of conducting my Oratorio at your Society.

The feeling of the Committee of Birminghan appears to be the same on the subject, *although they admitted that they had no right in preventing me from conducting it elsewhere;* and as I do not like to hurt their feelings, I prefer to be alone the loser, and make for them a sacrifice which, I assure you, is extremely painful to me.

Should it be possible that your performance could be postponed till the Saturday after the Birmingham Festival (the 22nd of September), I should be able to conduct, and it would be a true pleasure for me if this could be the case. But if it cannot be postponed to that day, and must stand for the Tuesday before the Festival, I beg you will receive my regrets for not being able to do as I should have wished, and present to the committee of your Society my sincere thanks for the honor they did me, and my most heartfelt regrets for the loss of pleasure I feel in declining their kind and honoring offers.

I have the honor to be, Sir, your obedient servant,

FELIX MENDELSSOHN-BARTHOLDY.

Extract from a letter of Mendelssohn's, printed in the Report, alluding to the composer's presence at the performance of " Elijah," which he was not allowed to conduct:

" I can hardly express the gratification I felt in hearing my work performed in so beautiful a manner; indeed, I shall never wish to hear some parts of it better executed than they were last night.

" The power of the choruses—this large body of good and musical voices—and the style in which they sang the whole of my music, gave me the highest and most heartfelt treat, while I thought on the immense improvement which such a number of *real* amateurs must necessarily produce in the country which may boast of it. It is for these gratifying feelings I wish to express my thanks to the committee of this Sciety, and I shall never forget the manner in which they performed my Oratorio, and the kind and most honoring reception I met with by the Sacred Harmonic Society."

14.

To T. Brewer, Esq., Hon. Sec. to the Sacred Harmonic Society, Exeter Hall, London.

[Written in English.]

LEIPZIG, October 7, 1846.

DEAR SIR: I beg to express my best thanks for the letter dated September 24, and it gives me much pleasure that the Sacred Harmonic Society will undertake the first performance of my " Elijah " before a London audience. I beg to thank the committee most sincerely for their flattering intention, and of course should be most happy to conduct the work myself on such an occasion, if I can come to London in April next. I hope and trust that I may have that pleasure, and that nothing may prevent me from doing so. But I am still doubtful, and cannot give a positive promise as far as regards my coming over; and as for the parts which you wish to have as soon as possible, I shall speak to the editor of them, Mr. Buxton, who, I hear, is expected shortly in Leipzig, and will ask him to let you have them as soon as they can be ready.

With many thanks to yourself and the Society, believe me, dear Sir, your very obedient servant,

FELIX MENDELSSOHN-BARTHOLDY.

15.

To Mr. Bartholomew.

[Written in English.]

LEIPZIG, January 20, 1847.

MY DEAR MR. BARTHOLOMEW: A happy new year to you, (although it is rather old already,) and many thanks for your kind and precious letter. Indeed, nobody could have written it but you, and nobody could have taken so much trouble with my choruses to the "Athalie" but you, and to nobody could I feel so sincerely and heartily indebted but to you.

Have many many thanks, my dear Sir, and be sure that you confer all these obligations on one who knows how to value them, and who will always remain thankful to you.

With these lines you receive the choral parts of the "Œdipus," which you wished to have. Of two of my favorite choruses I have made the P.F. arrangement, and send it to you, in order that you may see what they are meant for; the rest is, as you wanted it, quite without accompaniment. I hope you will accept of them, such as they are, and think of me when you peruse them. As for the stories of the Exeter Hall people,* I have written my mind at length to Mr. Buxton, and asked him to communicate my letter to you, and talk the thing over with you, and I shall be very happy to hear your advice.

The second part of "Elijah" will in a very short time be in Mr. Buxton's hands. And now, my dear Sir, let me repeat to you my heartfelt thanks for all you did again for me when they performed the "Athalie" choruses, and for your interesting report of all the proceedings before and during that performance, and for all the kindness and friendship which you always show me.

Always very truly and sincerely yours,

FELIX MENDELSSOHN-BARTHOLDY.

---

* What he terms "stories of the Exeter Hall people" relate to reports current at that time about Mendelssohn having undertaken to write an Opera for Mr. Lumley of Her Majesty's Theater. It was asserted to be the "Tempest" to a French libretto. This, and other reports of a like nature, caused the directors of the Sacred Harmonic Society to fear that he would not be ready with the "Elijah," which was to be performed in the ensuing spring under his *bâton.—Note by Mrs. Bartholomew.*

16.

To Mr. Bartholomew.

[Written in English.]

LEIPZIG, March 10, 1847.

MY DEAR SIR: Many thanks for your letter of the 1st. I really do not know what a synopsis of the Oratorio should be good for : on the other hand, I do not see the harm it could do, and therefore leave it to you to decide this point as you think best. I shall send you the metronomes in a few days ; the organ part I do not forget.

But tell me, should the whole series of performances not be better postponed till *autumn?* What with your uncertainty about Staudigl, and with all this uproar in London about the two opera parties, and with Jenny Lind coming or not coming, and with the " Tempest " or not the " Tempest," and with the difficulty you and Mr. Buxton have to make the parts ready,* would not such a delay be beneficial to all of us, especially to the old prophet himself? Not to me, certainly, who like to shake my English friends by the hand the sooner the better, but to all others. And now many thanks for your friendly advice in the opera affair. Some time before you wrote your letter to me, I had already informed Mr. Lumley that I should not be able to produce an Opera of the " Tempest " in the season 1847 ; and accord-

---

* None but the chorus parts were printed for the first performance at Birmingham. When this letter was written, the whole work was being published with the extensive alterations made by the composer: one of them being " Lift thine eyes," which was substituted for a duet.—*Note by Mrs Bartholomew.*

ing to the advice my friend Klingemann gave me some days before your letter came, I have since again written to Mr. Lumley (about the same words as you suggest), and have asked Klingemann to take care of seeing the letter safely delivered, and have sent to him a duplicate of it. So that the whole of your advice, the same which my friend K. gave, has been followed literally, and I should be very glad if thus the affair would come to an end. Of this I think I may be sure, that Mr. Lumley will not continue his advertisements of my Opera after he heard that I had taken the resolution *not to write* the " Tempest," for the season 1847.

The chorus " Grausam ist es, O Freund," although I have composed the music for it, was not performed at Berlin, and therefore was not in the score I gave to the copyist. If you wish to have it also, I will send it directly I hear from you. And now forgive this dry letter, and believe me, yours very truly,

FELIX MENDELSSOHN-BARTHOLDY.

No. III.

LETTERS TO JOSEPH MOORE, Esq.

1.

To Joseph Moore, Esq.

[Written in English.]   LEIPZIG, July 21, 1840.

MY DEAR SIR: I delayed the answer to your letters so long, because my health as well as that of my wife was not in a very good state, which made me feel uncertain whether I could stand the fatigues of such a great Festival as yours, and such a hasty journey home as I had three years ago—(for again I must be in Leipzig at the beginning of October, when our concert season opens). My physician would not even allow me to go some weeks ago, and wanted to send me to some of our baths; but now I am so much improved that he has changed his mind, and given his sanction to my journey, and I shall therefore come and have the pleasure of assisting at your Festival. The period of my arrival I cannot yet fix upon; it depends on my wife's health, which is not yet quite settled. If she can go with me, I shall come to England in the middle of next month; if I must go alone, I shall leave Leipzig not before September, and spend only a week before the Festival in London. I am afraid this last will be the case, although I should lose the greatest part of the pleasure I anticipated if I must come alone. Pray, my dear Sir, accept our best thanks for your kind and hospitable offers; I wish and hope still we might be able to accept them; but if not, you know our thanks and gratitude are the same, as your kindness is the same.

The composition which we performed here at the Festival, and which you want to have for the second day, is not, as you call it, a little Oratorio, its plan being not dramatic, but merely lyrical. It is called in German, " The Song of Praise," and consists of an instrumental symphony of three movements, which leads to a great chorus, to which twelve other vocal pieces, solos, and choruses succeed. Its time of duration is an hour and a quarter. I hope it will do for the second morning, but it must not begin the concert. I beg you will let it either conclude the first part, *or* (and this I would prefer by far) make it alone the last part of the performance. I do not know whether " The Song of Praise " is good English and a good title, and whether a better translation of our " Lobgesang " might not be found; of this I will soon write you more. I have found here an Englishman who translates the words for me. I preferred this, because I can always tell which parts I am able to alter, and which not; and if the task is done, I shall send it to my friends in England to look over and alter it, as they like. I write to-day to Novello, who can have the parts as soon as I get his answer; at all events, I have plenty of

parts, which I can bring with me, our Leipzig orchestra
having been a very great one. So much for the second
morning. On the 4th you mention another piece of
mine. I should like it to be either the "42nd Psalm,"
which is published in England, or the "114th Psalm,"
which is still MS., for a Double Chorus. The last is
very short, only fifteen minutes' duration; the former
the double of it; choose which you like best. On the
first morning I will perform something of Sebastian
Bach's on the organ; on the fourth something of my
composition. I am not sure whether I shall complete
my concerts in time for your Festival; I hope so, but if
not, I will perform something else on the pianoforte. If
you wish it, I will also bring over my new Overture,
with all the parts. If I make a stay in London before
your Festival, I have an idea of giving a concert for the
benefit of some charity there. I hope the Committee
will not oppose such an undertaking on the ground of
my first appearance being looked for at the Birmingham
Festival. Should such a feeling exist, I beg you will let
me know it immediately. Pray do not forget to answer
this point. Tell me also who your principal singers
and performers are, and who conducts the Festival.
Which soprano is to sing the solo part in my "Lobgesang" the second morning? I must have a very good
one, if possible. And pray keep to the idea of having a
rehearsal of it in London before the general rehearsal at
Birmingham; else it would be impossible for the best
band or chorus to do it with spirit and energy. Once

more, my own and my wife's best thanks for all your kindness, and believe me to remain very truly yours,

FELIX MENDELSSOHN-BARTHOLDY.

2.

To Joseph Moore, Esq.

[Written in English.]

FRANKFORT, July 21, 1845.

MY DEAR SIR: Have many thanks for your very kind and welcome letter, which I received a few days ago, and pray tell the members of the Committee for the next Festival how truly indebted I feel to them for the honor they have done me in inviting me to come over to their meeting next year.

I hope nothing shall prevent me to accept of so flattering and honorable an invitation, and beg to thank the committee and yourself, my dear Sir, most sincerely for it.

You know with how great a pleasure I have always visited your country; the prospect of doing so again affords always a true gratification to me, and your kind and hospitable invitation greatly adds to the pleasure I may thus anticipate. I have only to wish, then, that nothing may occur to prevent me from accepting so much kindness; for it is indeed a long time—more than a year—for settling any plans. Pray let me know at what time you would wish to have a positive and decided answer—I mean at what time you would consider my answer as an engagement which could not be altered on any account; and let me also know what you mean in saying that I am to assist you in selecting music, conducting and directing as much as possible. As for selecting, of course I shall be most happy to offer any advice which may be asked; but do you mean that I should have to conduct *all* the performances, or the *greater* part of them? · This, I fear, would be a task above my powers; but before I can say anything more on this subject, pray explain me what *your* meaning is, and name the period about which I asked you before.

Since some time I have begun an Oratorio,* and hope I shall be able to bring it out for the first time at your Festival; but it is still a mere beginning, and I cannot yet give you any promise as to my finishing it in time.

I have written to Mr. Webb some months ago, to tell him that I had already begun to work on another subject, and that I could not avail myself of his poem for that reason, much as I regretted it. If my Oratorio should be ready in time (as I hope it will), there would be no occasion for any other 'things of mine at the morning performances; but if I should not be able to finish it, I have several other things of mine which I could propose in its stead, either for the morning or evening concerts.

The " Œdipus " (which is to be performed next month at Potsdam) will scarcely do for any concert, I am afraid; but, as I said, I have other things.

---

* "Elijah."

I hear with much pleasure that you still go on with improvements in your splendid organ; but if I shall play it with pleasure, I must have a lighter touch, and broader keys in the pedals than what I found there last year. I am sure the pedals from C up to D (*two octaves and a note*) are quite enough, and it could then be contrived that the keys have the breadth which feet and boots usually require. And as for the heavy touch, I am sure that I admired your organist very much who was able to play a Fugue on them. I am afraid I would not have strength enough to do so, without a very long previous practice. Perhaps you may speak to Mr. Hill of these observations, and hear what he says to them.

How happy I should have been to see you on the Rhine, and in my country again! But I am sorry to say we could not meet unless you extended your journey further on to the interior of Germany. I leave the Rhine in a few days, and go for a time to Berlin (to the rehearsals of the "Œdipus"), and then to Leipzig, where I shall most probably stay the whole winter. It would be a great pleasure indeed to see you in those parts, but I am afraid it is out of the question, after what you say of the journey to the Rhine.

If you write, pray direct your letter henceforth to *Leipzig;* but if you come yourself—how much better that would be! You should have a glorious concert at Leipzig, and the most hearty welcome, I assure you.

Believe me always, very truly yours,
FELIX MENDELSSOHN-BARTHOLDY.

3.

To Joseph Moore, Esq.

[Written in English.]

Leipzig, October 19, 1845.

My Dear Sir: I received your first letter after an absence of a few weeks, and should have answered it long ago, for you know with how much pleasure I read it, and how truly indebted I felt to you and the committee for continuing your very kind feeling toward me! But I was uncertain which answer I had to give to some of the most important points, and this uncertainty is 'still the same; yet I must write, as I receive to-day your second letter, which shows your wish to have an immediate answer.

The principal point about which I am uncertain is whether I shall be able to have my new Oratorio ready in time for your Festival. There would have been no doubt of it, had I been able to continue my work quietly at Frankfort, as I began it. But now there are so many businesses here, at Dresden, at Berlin, which took up all my leisure time during the last months, that I have not been able to go on with it. If the businesses continue as they have begun (which, however, I hope they will not), I *shall not* be able to finish my Oratorio in time. If they do *not* continue, I *shall* finish it in time. But during this uncertainty I am not able to make an engagement as to the first performance of this work.

The second point is that I am afraid I shall not be strong enough to go through the office of being sole con-

ductor of the morning performances at such a Festival
as yours is. In former years I had only to conduct my
compositions, not the other pieces of your programme;
and yet I recollect how excited and fatigued I always
felt after the Festival was over. Therefore I hesitate to
accept of the honor which you intend doing me, and
which I fear I should not be able to go through, although
I sincerely wished it.

The question now is whether you would want me yet
(to come to the Festival without having a certainty as
to these two points, and even with the possibility of my
answering them at last in the negative), or whether you
consider them as so essential that the whole idea of my
coming over (much as I would regret it) must be given
up with them.

I beg you will give me an answer to this question as
soon as you conveniently can. If the first should be
the case (and I hope you fully know how glad I should
be to see you again, and to come), I would set at work
as hard as I could whenever any leisure is left me to
finish my new piece, and at any rate I should propose
several others (although not so extensive ones) for the
morning performances. But if the second should be the
case, I sincerely hope and trust you would be convinced
of my deep regret, and would allow me another year to
enjoy of an honor and a treat which I should have been
obliged to give up so much against my wishes this
time. Be it as it may, I beg you will present my best
and most sincere thanks to the committee, and I beg

you will think of me, my dear Sir, as of one who shall *always* feel true gratitude and thankfulness for all the kindness and friendship you have shown to him! All my family are well, thank God, and unite in best wishes for your perfect health and happiness. I hope now soon to hear again from you, and am, my dear Sir, very truly yours,

FELIX MENDELSSOHN-BARTHOLDY.

4.

To Joseph Moore, Esq.

[Written in English.

LEIPZIG, December 11, 1845.

MY DEAR SIR: Many thanks for your very kind letter. I have now made up my mind to come to Birmingham in August; but I wish to conduct only my own music, as in former years, and have nothing to do with the other parts of the programme. I cannot yet give any promise as to my new Oratorio, but in a month or two I shall be able to tell you for certain whether, and when, I can send it. If I cannot, I would try to propose something else of my new music. You want something, whether new or old, for the Friday: would the "Walpurgisnacht" do for it? I conducted it only once in England, at the last Philharmonic, 1844, and they seemed to like it then. Or would the music to the "Midsummer Night's Dream" be the thing? My Symphony in A minor, about which you questioned me in one of your former letters, lasts about thirty five to forty minutes.

And if you can have Jenny Lind for the Festival, by all means have her, for we have now no singer on the Continent who is to be compared to her. But although she has no fixed engagement, neither at Berlin nor elsewhere, I fear it will be difficult to make her come, as they are all mad about her, and force her into more engagements than she can accept. And Pischek would also be the man, I am sure! But he is known already in England, and if you get Jenny Lind, it will be such a novelty at the same time, and will give a new character to the Festival. Now, before all, I hope that these lines may find you in better health, that your indisposition will be forgotten long before they arrive, and that I may meet you again in perfect strength and happiness! With my wife's and family's best regards, believe me always to remain, my dear Sir, yours very truly,

FELIX MENDELSSOHN-BARTHOLDY.

5.

To Joseph Moore, Esq.

[Written in English.]

LEIPZIG, January 17, 1846.

MY DEAR SIR: Yesterday I received your letter of the 7th, and answer it as early as I can. My Oratorio is in progress, and becomes every day more developed; but whether I shall be able to finish it in time for your preparations is another question, which I shall not be able to answer positively before *two months* are elapsed. It will then be the middle of March, more than five

11

months before the period of your Festival, and if I should fail in my efforts of ending my work in time (which I fully hope and trust to do), there will be ample time for you to make it up by something else. Your question about Jenny Lind is very important to the success of the Festival, as I consider her, without hesitation, as the first singer of the day, and perhaps of many days to come. But I am not able to undertake the negotiation which your chairman would intrust me with, as I know how much she is surrounded with engagements of all sorts, and how little likely it is that I could get anything like a positive answer from her, unless a formal application from the committee had previously been made to her. It is by no means certain that such an application would be successful, but at any rate I think it the only way, if there is one. When you formally wrote to me about the same subject, I was at Berlin, and spoke to her about it; but then she said she should not go to England, she had declined it already twice; it was quite impossible, etc., etc.; so that I am sure that she will not come to *London* at least (for I did not make any direct inquiries about Birmingham and the Festival at that time). When you have determined what you will do, and if you have written, or if another (perhaps at Berlin) has negotiated for you, pray let me know of it, and I could then perhaps be of some use in removing some difficulties which might still arise, and in persuading her to accept the Festival, which I should be most happy to do. But at present, I am afraid, by beginning to talk or correspond with Jenny Lind about this subject, I would do your cause no good, and I therefore beg to be excused.

My opinion about the new text to the "Mount of Olives," which you kindly want to have, is that this music certainly must have a different translation from what is usually done, and that even for several of the concerted pieces there ought to be written a different poetry, the sense of the German words being contrary to your religious feelings on the subject (as well as to mine, and I may say to *ours*): I mean particularly those pieces in which Christ is introduced as a tenor solo with concerted pieces, arias, etc. But I should *strongly recommend* not to take a poetry which *entirely* changes the subject, and which makes a David in the wilderness of the Mount of Olives. *I do not know one specimen* of such an attempt having been successful, and I think I could *prove* it to be *impossible*. Besides, this music and its meaning is already too much known, and too many amateurs are aware of the signification of every piece; they would never be pleased with such an alteration, and it would produce a doubtful if not disagreeable sensation. Perhaps the best way would be to introduce, instead of Christ and St. Peter, merely voices like those of witnesses of all these things—relating the events historically, not dramatically, and removing entirely the idea of an Opera in which these holiest names are introduced. But it would require a very skillful poet indeed to make even these alterations.

And now, many many good wishes for your health and happiness in this year, and in very many more to come, and always believe me to remain, my dear Sir, truly and sincerely yours,

FELIX MENDELSSOHN-BARTHOLDY.

G.

To Joseph Moore, Esq.

[Written in English.]

LEIPZIG, May 8, 1846.

MY DEAR SIR: I write these lines to inform you that I intend to send the whole of the first part of my Oratorio to Mr. Moscheles in the course of the next fortnight. It is by far the greater part of the two; the choruses from the second part will be in England toward the beginning of July, and the rest of the whole in the middle of that month. All this, "Deo volente."

I wish Mr. Bartholomew, in London, who has translated several other vocal pieces of mine, would undertake also this, and I wish he might take advice of my friend Mr. Klingemann, who understands both languages thoroughly, and who understands my music better than both languages.

The most essential condition for my Oratorio is a most excellent baritone singer—a man like Pischek, or Staudigl, or Oberhofer. Will you have such a m . .

[Here the letter is torn away, and concluded in a lady's handwriting, thus:]

Believe me always yours truly,

FELIX MENDELSSOHN-BARTHOLDY.

7.

To Joseph Moore, Esq.

[Written in English.]

Leipzig, August 2, 1846.

My Dear Sir : I hear this moment from Mr. Moscheles that you are anxious to know what becomes of me and of my Oratorio. I therefore hasten to inform you (although I am sure you will have heard it before this arrives) that the last portion of the Oratorio, except a song which I bring over with me, was some time ago sent off to London, and that the instrumental parts have been copied here, the numbers being as you indicated in your letter. I shall make a rehearsal of these parts on *Wednesday next* with the orchestra HERE, (although I have not one vocal part,) in order to save the English artists the time of correcting faults which may be found here, and to make the rehearsals there as short as possible. And I hope to be in London on the 17th, and shortly afterward at Birmingham, and I hope to find you in good health and happiness, and very glad am I to shake hands with you again! Always very truly yours,

Felix Mendelssohn-Bartholdy.

8.

To Joseph Moore, Esq.

[Written in English.]

Leipzig, September 28, 1846.

My Dear Sir: I have now returned home, found all my family as well as I might have wished ; and while I think over the events of this last journey, I cannot help addressing these few lines to you, in order to express once more the most sincere and most heartfelt thanks for your very kind reception, and for the friendship you have again shown to me during my stay at your house. Indeed, the first performance of my " Elijah " exceeded all the wishes which the composer may feel at such an important moment, and the evident good-will of all the artists in the orchestra, as well as the kindness with which the audience received the work, will be as long as I live a source of grateful recollection. And yet it seems to me that I should not have enjoyed so great a treat as thoroughly and intensely as I did, if it had not been for your kindness and continued friendship, and for the comfortable home which you offered to me during those days of excitement. Our quiet morning and evening conversations with Mr. Ayrton and Mr. Webb are to my mind quite connected with the performances at the Town Hall, and form an important part of *my* Musical Festival at Birmingham ; and while I should certainly never have assisted at one of them if it had not been for our very old acquaintance, and while I accordingly owe to you the whole of the treat which this first performance of " Elijah " affords me, I must at the same time thank you no less heartily and sincerely for the quiet and comfortable stay, and the friendly reception at your house, which enhanced all those pleasures so considerably. That your health may now be quite restored again after the fatigues you have undergone, and that

we may soon meet again (either in your country, or
once more in mine), and that you will continue the
same kindness and friendship which you have now
shown to me, and which I always met with from you
since so many years, is the most earnest wish and hope
of yours very truly and gratefully,

FELIX MENDELSSOHN-BARTHOLDY.

9.

To Joseph Moore, Esq.

[Written in English.]   MANCHESTER, April 21, 1847.

MY DEAR SIR: Many many thanks for your very kind
note and invitation, of which I shall be most happy to
avail myself. My time will be very limited, as I must
assist at the Philharmonic Concert in London on the 26th,
and conduct there my " Elijah " on the 28th again. I
shall therefore arrive at Birmingham on the 27th, just in
time to go to the Town Hall, and rehearse at half-past
one, and must leave Birmingham on the next day at half-
past nine. Now, if you will allow me, I shall come to
your house *immediately* after the rehearsal, and I hope
that we may have a quiet chat after the concert, or the
next morning, and that I may then again thank you for
all your kindness, present and past.

Always very truly yours,

FELIX MENDELSSOHN-BARTHOLDY.

No. IV.

EXTRACTS FROM

LETTERS ON ORGAN MUSIC, Etc.

Extracts from letters of Mendelssohn to the late Mr Coventry, music publisher, (written in the English language), on the subject of organ music—Bach's Organ pieces, *edited by Mendelssohn*, and Organ Sonatas, *written by Mendelssohn.*

1.

Frankfort, August 29, 1844.

According to your wishes, I send you a copy of the whole of my collection of my organ pieces by Seb. Bach, which I have carefully looked over and corrected. (1) 15 grand choral Preludes; (2) 44 little choral Preludes; (3) 6 Variations; (4) 11 Variations; (5) 4 Preludes and Fugues. Of the last I think several (if not all) have already been published in Germany or England. Both the Variations, I believe, have never been published, as also the greatest part of the 44 and of the 15 Preludes. Perhaps 9 out of these 59 are known; all the rest are not.

. . . .

I have also been very busy about the organ pieces, and they are nearly finished. I should like to call them,

"3 *Sonatas* for the Organ," instead of *Voluntaries*.
Tell me if you like this title as well; if not, I think the
name of Voluntaries will suit the pieces also, the more
so as I do not know what it means precisely.

2.

Pray alter the inscription which is to be found at the
bottom of every page, *Fugues, etc.* Why is Bach's name
always connected with Fugues? He has had more to
do with Psalm-tunes than with Fugues; and you call
the beginning of your collection Bach's Studies, which
I like much better. Pray alter this, and call it either
Studies, Organ pieces, or Chorales, or as you like. but
not Fugues. Let me know before it is issued, the title
which the work is to have in English: perhaps you
will send me a copy of it with the next proofs.

.   .   .   .   .   .

I hope to send you soon the promised organ pieces.
9 are ready, but I want to have 12 before I make a parcel of them.

3.

As a title, I should propose : " John Sebastian Bach's
Organ Composition on Chorales (Psalm-tunes), edited
by Felix M.-B. Vols. I. and II.: 44 Short Preludes; vols.
III. and IV.: 16 Grand Preludes; Vol. V.: 2 Chorales
with Variations." But, as for this title as well as for the

preface, I make it *a condit'on* that you submit them first to my friend Klingemann, and get his " imprimatur," as I dare not appear before the English public without this sanction.

4.

May 1, 1845.

I beg you will let me know whether a letter, which I wrote to you some weeks since, has reached you or not. It contained the communication that I had written a kind of Organ-school in six Sonatas for that instrument, and the question whether you would like to have the whole work or only one-half of it.

5.

May 26, 1845.

I duly received your favor of the 29th April, and, as I have no objection to your dividing my Sonatas into two books, I was very glad to see that they are to appear altogether at your house. I even think it would be well to sell each Sonata separately, if somebody wants to have them so; but it must always be with the title of: " Six Sonatas, etc., Nos. 1, 2, etc." Pray, if you place it into the engraver's hands, let him be most careful, in order to get a correct edition. I attach much importance to these Sonatas (if I may say so of any work of mine), and accordingly wish them to be brought out as correctly as possible. Perhaps some one of my English friends and brother organ-players would look them over for me (besides the usual corrections of the proofs).

6.

August 8, 1845.

You will see that, in the Prelude and Fugue in G major (particularly in the Prelude), I have made a great many corrections ; this is owing to my having seen a new edition of this piece which appeared some months ago (at Peters', Leipzig, and Ewer's, London), and in which the editor says he has had Bach's autograph as an authority. Accordingly, I adopted many readings which I thought evidently better than those of my copy, although this may have been taken from another autograph of Bach's (as he used to copy out his own things, and introduce alterations in every new copy).

7.

LEIPZIG, March 20, 1846.

I send the proofs of the Bach through a correspondent at Hamburgh to you, and hope you will duly receive them. If the faults which I corrected are carefully taken out, I am sure it will be a good edition. Pray be sure that, instead of " per organ piano," there should stand everywhere " per organ pieno." I wrote down a few observations to serve as a preface to the 15 grand choral Vorspiele ; but I was not able to translate them into good English, and I therefore send the German, and beg you will ask somebody to translate it. But I should like to see the English version before it is published.

No. V.

LETTER FROM M. F. DAVID

TO

DR. STERNDALE BENNETT.

—

Leipzig, November 25, 1847.

MY DEAREST FRIEND: I have just received your letter, which, from the proofs it contains of your continued friendship, has caused me the greatest joy. But it has also deeply affected me. Yes, we have indeed suffered an irreparable loss. How shall I attempt to draw a picture for you of this recent melancholy period! This summer in Baden and in Switzerland I found Mendelssohn bowed down with sorrow for the death of his sister. After he had in some degree recovered from the first shock, he began to work, and, as his wife tells me, with almost feverish zeal—to which, indeed, the very many works he has left, begun during the summer, bear testimony. After having composed without intermission day after day, he was in the habit of passing many days in succession rambling over the mountains, returning home much sunburnt and exhausted, when he would at once begin again to compose: in short, he was in the greatest state of excitement. After his return here (to Leipzig), he was certainly in a very serious mood; still there were days when he was quite cheerful, till he went one day to see Frau Frege, when, after she had sung, to the piano, his newest songs, all of a melancholy nature, he was seized with his first attack of illness. At first no great importance was attached to this, although the symptoms (hands and feet as cold as ice, stoppage of pulse, and some hours of delirium) were alarming enough. But as he had once a similar attack here seven years ago, from which he quickly recovered, none of us dreaded anything very serious. I saw him some daysa fterward, and found him again in good spirits, although he said to me, "1 feel as if some one were lying on the watch for me, and saying *Stop! no further!*" ("Halt! nicht weiter!") Twelve days after the first seizure, I was with him between eleven and twelve o'clock; he was very cheerful, and intended to set off to Vienna in a few days. His second attack of illness occurred in the afternoon, but he rallied from it also; so, though now very uneasy, we were not wholly dispirited, until a third attack came on seven days after the second, which he only survived till the evening of the following day. Never can I forget Gade coming to me at the Conservatorium to say Mendelssohn had been seized afresh with illness, and that it was now a question of life and death. I instantly rushed out, and was received by the intelligence that all hope was over. I was obliged to wait for a quarter of an hour before being sufficiently composed to go into his room. He was quite unconscious (this was on Wednesday evening), and cried out terribly till about ten o'clock. He then began to make sounds of instruments with his lips, as if music was haunting his brain; when exhausted by this, he again uttered a cry of anguish, and remained in the same state all through the night. The pain seemed to diminish during the course of the day, but his face was already that of a dying man; at a quarter after nine o'clock in the evening, he died! The most gentle and placid smile overspread his features. I will not speak of myself; you can feel with me, and with us all what we have lost in him. His admirable wife is composed, and bears with touching, pious resignation the sad bereavement with which God has afflicted her. I mean to go to her to-morrow, to let her know the faithful sympathy with which you think of her. How I rejoice to hear that the sorrow is so universal with you; Leipzig and London have indeed only that one point in common—the highest reverence for Mendelssohn. How much I should rejoice to see you here; do carry your plan into execution. It is not probable that I shall come to London. I could scarcely do so, totally devoid of all musical objects; and *with* these, it would be rather a burden than a recreation to me. My wife is well, and also my five children. Your little god-child (born on Mendelssohn's birthday) is very thriving. I will deliver all your messages. Write to me soon again. You say nothing of your wife; no doubt she is quite well. Pray give her my kind regards, and continue your affection for your attached and loving friend,

FERDINAND DAVID.